Queen of Heaven

by Jose Mercado Ventura

© Copyright 2023 Jose Mercado Ventura

ISBN 979-8-88824-168-4

All rights reserved. No part of this publication may be reproduced, stored in a retrieval system, or transmitted in any form or by any means—electronic, mechanical, photocopy, recording, or any other—except for brief quotations in printed reviews, without the prior written permission of the author.

This is a work of fiction. All the characters in this book are fictitious, and any resemblance to actual persons, living or dead, is purely coincidental. The names, incidents, dialogue, and opinions expressed are products of the author's imagination and are not to be construed as real.

Published by

◣köehlerbooks™

3705 Shore Drive
Virginia Beach, VA 23455
800-435-4811
www.koehlerbooks.com

QUEEN
of
HEAVEN

Jose Mercado Ventura

VIRGINIA BEACH
CAPE CHARLES

For the muses that inspire us.

TABLE OF CONTENTS

Chapter 1: A Way to Escape the Pain?..................5

Chapter 2: Shadow Boxing Demons..................11

Chapter 3: Stripped of Dignity..................20

Chapter 4: Reprieve..................29

Chapter 5: Onward to the Red Planet..................37

Chapter 6: Martian Monotony..................48

Chapter 7: The Ability to Love Again..................56

Chapter 8: Eudaimonia..................68

Chapter 9: When Worlds Collide..................76

Chapter 10: Love in Our Golden Years..................97

Chapter 11: Vacation on Olympus Mons..................105

Chapter 12: The Sands of Time..................116

Chapter 1

A WAY TO ESCAPE THE PAIN?

"LAST CALL TO board flight 456 from Crystal City Spaceport to Aerolis, Mars. Last call." Those words were carried throughout the halls of the Spaceport to the drop-off area just before the entrance gates. Even in the midst of all the frenzy of people bustling, coming from or going to their destinations, sending off loved ones, and the large staff keeping the facility alive and running, the announcement made its way outside. Even those who were motionless and led by curiosity, fascination, or whim, leaning on the large windows to get a glimpse of the rockets taking off—not even their presence was enough to trap the sound waves carrying the last announcement for the next departure. The announcement prevailed in all the traffic pouring into the Spaceport and drop-off area, despite engines revving, horns blaring, and the shouts and arguments between those in a rush. Finally, the air still managed to carry the sound, reverberating louder than in the Spaceport halls and lingering in the ears, causing dissonance and regret in a would-be passenger who hesitated at the last moment

"Five, four, three, two, one! We have liftoff!" said an announcer over the intercom.

"Estimated arrival time for flight 456 to Aerolis is five months. Departure for Providence Lunar Space Colony set for T-minus four hours. We thank you for choosing Crystal City Intergalactic Spaceport..."

Sigh. Guess there's always next time, thought the reluctant man.

The heat haze and fire coming out of the rocket thrusters blended with and distorted the sunset sky, giving the illusion that the ship was moving with no propulsion of its own but by an upward gravity. Although space travel has been common and frequent for quite some time, many are still awed by the beauty and majesty of a rocket taking off, stopping whatever they're doing and turning their attention toward any rocket in proximity. In 2092, people all throughout Earth enjoy the luxury of seeing these spacecrafts at various times throughout the day, with the clockwork schedule of ships transporting travelers, goods, and supplies to the lunar and Martian colonies, as well as the commercial pit stops scattered in between; if one were to miss a launch, there would be much consolation when another quickly followed. The convenience of traveling to Mars left the impression that there was no need to rush to start a new life on Mars in the hesitant passenger's mind; there was always another seat to buy and another time to fully commit. And like the previous times of not committing to the trip, the hesitant passenger started his car and headed back home.

The quiet ride back left endless time and room for his mind to reflect. The man was disappointed, not just in himself, for passing up yet another opportunity, but even on a handsome salary, a ticket to Mars was quite expensive. *Money,* he thought to himself, *money that could have been spent on better liquor.* He made sure there was enough to make going back home bearable, numbing himself before reaching blotto and passing out. Stumbling out of his car, he felt good entering his apartment building, keeping his concentration in hopes of pressing the right button for his floor. The elevator took him up to his loft, a total of twenty-five seconds to reach the top of the forty-story building, one of many buildings downtown competing for control of the skyline. *If I could just muffle the relentless, torturous thoughts that play like a feedback loop and make it through another night, hope may come in the morning,* he thought, shutting the front door behind him.

"Where the hell have you been, Mike?" Steven said as Michael settled inside, still in an intoxicated state.

"You don't pick up anybody's calls. Everybody at work is looking for you. I had to stall and cover for you, and believe me, it was not easy canceling my appointments to see your patients," Steven said as Michael settled in, leaving his shoes at the front door.

Still in a euphoric state, Michael was having a little difficulty setting his shoes on the rack, setting aside his cane, and balancing the bags he received from the kind attendant at the liquor store in both arms. While at the rack, Michael's eyes kept drifting but focused just long enough to glimpse himself in the mirror by the front door.

There was a huge grin staring back at him, reminding him of patients' looks fresh out of an operation, high on propofol and other anesthetics. It also made him wonder how he managed to drive back home in one piece. He tried so hard to keep his composure, but seeing the inebriated look on his face made him burst out in laughter. In this dream-like state, Michael could barely see and hear Steven through the blurry filter shrouding his senses.

"Make yourself at home," said Michael as he placed the bags on a kitchen counter.

"Jesus Christ! Are you drunk? Did you drink and drive?" said Steven.

"What the hell do you care?"

"Yeah, you're right. I don't care," Steven said sarcastically, "but I'd have a hard time letting your family know that their son made the obituary column. And Christ, imagine having to be me, explaining to your mother that her beloved baby boy was dead. You know how overprotective she is. She'd lose her shit."

"They have their own lives to worry about, as do I."

Michael made his way to the living room couch. There was a brief silence. The energy in the room started to get gloomy, and the blank stare in Michael's face got Steven more concerned.

"You still haven't answered. Where were you, man?"

"I was right there. Ticket in hand. All I had to do was board the flight."

"This again? What is this, like the fourth time this year?"

"You don't understand."

"I would if you just tell me what's the matter. You always have this sullen look on your face, and whenever anyone asks what's wrong, you hide and ignore everyone who cares about you. And whenever you seem to be in any sort of good mood, it's always accompanied with the stench of booze. Tell me, man. Just get it out in the open."

"You already know what's wrong."

"Mike, Katherine has been gone for almost two years. You have got to let it go."

"I can't. She was the only person who truly loved me. She was the only woman who loved me. The only one who saw me as a human and loved me despite my flaws and my disease. While people would laugh at my limp and patronize me or see me as a mistake in the gene pool, she saw me as a good man. When she was around, the pain was gone. She was my placebo. She made all those memories of lonely nights fade away, gave me a reason to get up in the morning. She was beautiful inside and out. But now that she's gone, I don't see me really having a reason to stay here. I thought, maybe, maybe I could start a new life on Mars. Maybe the distance will make me forget her. I don't know. I just know I need to do something to get my mind off her because I'm afraid I might not be here or on Mars or anywhere else if you get what I'm saying, which is why I'm always sedating myself or contemplating something so drastic, like going into space."

"And engaging in reckless behavior!" Steven sat next to Michael on the sofa. "Pain bad?"

"Yeah. Fuck, I tell ya, when the pain is bad, it amplifies the loneliness and makes the sadness worse."

"You know that your family and friends support you, dude. You can always call me or Gabrielle. We are always here for you."

"Thanks."

"It's nothing. Also, you know you have the support of the other doctors and staff down at the hospital. If you need a new painkiller refill, I'll make sure you get one right away—no delays. Though I'm not sure why you don't upgrade your interface to sync up to your brain and have it block and release the medicine from there. But anyway, you need anything else, I'm your guy."

"You know why I don't have a chip in me. I'm old school with my regimen. And look, I know that you're trying to cheer me up, but it doesn't make me feel like I have anything worth living for."

"Don't have anything to live for? Are you kidding me? What you do for the patients at the hospital is incomparable to any other doctor—you go above and beyond. Who else can say they have an awesome car and this awesome loft with an incredible view of downtown?"

"It doesn't really matter to have material possessions if you're always alone and in pain."

"Don't you worry about being alone. I'm sure some great woman will come into your life. You just gotta keep your head up."

"No woman even looks in my direction. What are you talking about?"

"That's cause you're always looking down, drunk, or irritated. Just try and keep your mind off things. And we have got to get you out of this house and loving life again."

"As long as you don't force me to come to your meditation classes. I rather die than endure that insufferable New Age crap."

"Okay, okay. We'll go out somewhere more to your liking. I'll call you early tomorrow morning to make sure you come into work."

"Can't make it in tomorrow. I'll be too busy having a hangover."

"Alright, well then, I'll make sure you bring your ass in Wednesday. Okay?"

"Sure."

"Alright bro, take care, and I hope you feel better. Goodnight."

"Night," Michael said, biding Steven goodbye.

At 3 a.m., Michael lay quiet and still in his bed. He had just gotten up from a dream about Katherine filled with a happiness that reminded him of the times he spent with her. Though it was not a nightmare but a pleasant dream, not a hint of anything terrifying that would wake him from a deep sleep, it was exactly that—the content of happiness—that stirred up many past experiences and emotions they shared together. The false sense of reality that his subconscious mind tried to impress upon him that Katherine was alive and occupying the same time and space as him was sickening. How could his mind not erase the memories of Katherine? Katherine was made up of the same atoms as his mind. If her atoms, matter, and all that she was had disappeared, why didn't the same happen to the thoughts of her? It played with his mind, mocking him, like bait to a fish, waiting for him to bite, leaving him with hurt. But this was far worse than a nightmare; a nightmare could only compile the illogical, deep-seated fears of the psyche to display in nocturnal fantasy, but what his mind had orchestrated was a full-on psychological assault, using the very thing that he loved. What's worse is that he could not run away from his attacker—as it was the brain that kept him alive.

"Guess I didn't drink enough," Michael said. He turned to his nightstand, took out ten oxycodone tablets from the drawer, and washed it down with the remaining whiskey in his glass, waiting until he got sleepy. Maybe in another world, where all potentialities exist, they are happily together, and dreams are the mode by which he can travel to those places where Katherine is. He was happy that his mind gave that peaceful thought, even if it was a lie stemming from drugs and alcohol, and he was grateful for it. It left a smile on his face as he fell back asleep, and a tear of joy rolled down his cheek as he dreamt.

Chapter 2

SHADOW BOXING DEMONS

"SAY, 'AAAHHH.' GOOD. Everything seems to check out, Mr. Hamilton. Like I said, there was no need to show the lesion on your butt from earlier, though I do encourage my patients to tell me everything that raises alarm, so thanks for sharing," Michael said.

"So, it's nothing?"

"Not necessarily. If it doesn't improve and persists for longer than two weeks, I'd advise you to see your dermatologist. But my guess is, it's just an ingrown hair. Don't worry about it. In the meantime, remember to get your flu shots since the threat of catching a bug is more probable than cancer on your back end. If you'd like, I can arrange for one of the nurses to administer one right now."

"Sure, Doc."

"Okay, the nurse will be with you in just a moment. Now I must go. I'm late for a prearrangement. Just schedule another appointment if necessary, or if it's an emergency, just come back to the hospital. Take care."

"I know I volunteered, but why does the hospital keep assigning me to see patients with minor problems?" Michael said to the receptionist at the front desk. "I'm a research physician specializing in gene therapy, for Christ's sake. Save the cuts and boo-boos for the residents. I would imagine there would at least be a case that would require my expertise." He sighed. "Anyhow, Mr. Hamilton's chart is on file, and he needs a flu shot. If he schedules another clinic visit, see if you can give the appointment to someone else, will ya, Denise?"

"I'll do what I can, but Dr. Acosta, the patients you desire to see are given to your understudies. I guess the dean and committee feel you should be devoting all your time in the lab and not be overwhelmed by other burdens," Denise replied.

"Overwhelmed? More like they don't want to lose out on a potential breakthrough." Michael paused. "Do I look overwhelmed to you?"

Denise was hesitant and scrambling for words but was saved when a patient called to make an appointment. "Gotta take this call."

Michael checked his interface—fifteen minutes after five—and decided to leave the hospital to make it on time to his secret meeting. While exiting the hospital, he ran into an associate, Dr. Barbra Rosen, in the first-floor hall of the Seedfelt cancer ward. Dr. Rosen was head of that department and a member of the hospital committee, which provided Michael a chance to ask and clear any concerns he had regarding his job at the hospital.

"Honestly, Dr. Acosta, you always seem like you don't want to be here. You seem to be carrying around a huge burden. And there's a hint of alcohol under your breath at times. I think the hospital is just trying to keep you away from patients. But don't you worry your head about it. You're too good to get rid of, which is why I think they're so accommodating. If it was anyone else, they would have canned them already. If there's anything you need to discuss or you need time off, which you deserve, just let me know, will you?"

Michael nodded, expressed his gratitude for the concern, and bid her farewell. Michael checked his interface again—twenty-five minutes past five—and he was still on hospital grounds. Getting into his car, Michael got an email alert on his interface buzzing on his wrist. Being in a hurry, he was going to wait to open it, but the sender and subject caught his attention. It was a response from Parson's

Memorial Hospital regarding a résumé Michael sent them months before. The message said a new position at their internal medicine department was available, and they would be thrilled if he could join them. Michael was surprised; he was sure he would never hear back, given all the time that had passed. If accepted, the hospital would pay for travel and living expenses for the first year and a salary twice his current one. Looking at all the great details and perks, he rubbed his eyes to ensure he was reading it correctly, and while gathering himself together, he was still in disbelief that they responded. He had impulsively sent his résumé, reasoning with himself that he might as well have a job lined up that first time he planned to leave for Mars. *Funny*, he thought, *that a job he applied for and thought of as a joke responded with a serious offer.*

He laughed briefly, then saved the response on his interface, convinced the offer was persuasive enough to bookmark should he have to fully commit to a plan. The car was finally moving, and Michael raced through the downtown streets quickly, carefully maneuvering through traffic and crossing his fingers that the person he was meeting would still see him. Michael pulled up to the corner of Pike and Baileys and parked his car in front of the building's sidewalk. He disembarked and motion-swiped with his interface, putting enough money on the parking meter to last an hour. Since Michael was meeting in secret, he made sure he went around back, hoping no one saw him entering the building. Dr. Moss let Michael in and quickly went upstairs to his office. They had agreed to meeting in secret due to Michael not wanting anyone to know that he was seeking the help of a therapist.

The whole ordeal was unfamiliar for Michael, as he had never met with a shrink before, and there was an awkward silence in the room. He always thought only the insane needed therapy, afraid of having a label placed on him. Dr. Moss could sense Michael's slight reluctance and paced himself, looking for the right way to begin the conversation that would break down the guard that many first timers have when confronting their mental health.

"I'd like to start off by saying, first and foremost, welcome, Michael. It's a pleasure having you here. I know it must not be particularly easy going through all the trouble of seeing me here today," Dr. Moss said.

"You mean admitting I have deep, unresolved issues, convincing myself to seek help, and making sure I followed through coming to see you?" Michael said. They both laughed. "Seriously, though, Robert, thanks for agreeing to have me as an anonymous patient."

"It's nothing. I remember when we were residents at North Regional. We had each other's backs, alternating shifts so we could sleep during those thirty-six-hour marathons they had us running. Enduring that together, we'll be connected for life."

"Don't remind me. All those horrible experiences in the ER. Remember the time that old man took enough Viagra to forge a hammer, and right as the rookie was about to perform the aspiration, in comes the nurse and he came all over the place?"

He laughed. "I remember. They had to call in biohazard to clean up the place. Must've been the happiest day in a long time for that old man," Dr. Moss said.

"So, I see you're living well. Pretty snazzy office you got here. Guess you were right; psychiatry is where all the money is."

"I told your indecisive self that when you were hesitant to pick your subspecialty. But I think you made the right choice going into research. Your work, along with the other notable scientists', contributed to the perfecting of gene therapy. Now parents won't fear the burden of genetic disease, and existing patients with chronic diseases are essentially in remission. You did what you set out to do and kept the promise you made when you got into college—to find a cure or help find a cure for not just your disease but many diseases that had no effective therapies. Anyway, I'm sure you're doing well for yourself, doubling as a clinician and researcher."

"Yeah, I do pretty well, although I've been getting less

opportunities working as a physician in the clinic. The hospital is making sure the patients don't see a doctor with an 'unchipper' disposition—bad rep for the hospital, I'm guessing."

"Well, now, since you brought that up, I guess it is the best time to address the problems that brought you here."

"Where should I begin?"

"Start with whatever you feel comfortable talking about, though I always suggest to never hold back. The goal we're trying to reach here is resolution. I don't want to hear anything superficial. I need you to dive deep into the inner part of your being, the place in your mind that all the symptoms stem from. What is bothering you deep inside, Michael? Tell me. I'm all ears." There was a brief silence as Michael ruminated.

"Imagine, for a second, being born already at a disadvantage. You've heard the saying . . . the bottom dropping out. Well, for me, there was never a bottom to stand on. Metaphorically, I was born with the ocean at my neck. Great start, right? Family's poor. Your family comes from generational poverty and violence. Father is abusive, beats everyone; you, your mother, siblings, you grow up and are always in a state of fear and anxiety. You endure this for a good portion of your early life, but I tell ya, those days feel like several lifetimes when each hit from your old man struck. Father blames everyone for his actions and sees no wrong that he's done—still will not take the responsibility even to this day. But the good news is the waves must settle. And at some point, it becomes bearable when the water drops to waist level. Your family now consists of your mother, siblings, and you. You're now living in a relatively healthy environment—always moving like a nomad, but hey, you're safe, so that's all that matters.

"Nevertheless, the waves still must follow their cycle, just as all other systems in life, and soon, the tide returns, and now you're at eye level. At eleven years old, you fracture your foot. It's placed in a cast and declared healed, but you continue to have pain. Years and years go by, and no doctor can find a diagnosis, but it's fine, no cause for alarm because you're still functional. Then, and this is where it turns for the worse, after graduating high school, a couple months pass, and you can't walk anymore. You have no means to see a doctor, so you go untreated for years and writhe in pain, being bedridden and isolated from the world; then you drop to ninety-seven pounds. You're finally able to get medical attention after years of legal battles trying to prove your medical necessity for government healthcare. You remember how it was back in the late fifties and early sixties? Anyway, I digress. Two hip replacements and several years of ongoing and excruciating physical therapy later, you are now able to be mobile and functional on a barely competent level. Now, though you are in college, working toward your degree and profession, establishing yourself into the world again, you would think you wouldn't feel alone, I mean cause, hell, you went through seven years of isolation, right? But no, you feel even lonelier.

"Don't get me wrong. I thank you for being my friend, but I needed someone to be intimate with, a female with a kind presence to compliment my masculinity and human need for companionship. You dread going to bed. In bed, your mind loops, remembering all the people in love you saw that day, reminding you of the lack of it in your life, driving you mad. Don't fret, though, because something good happens, and a wonderful woman comes into your life to make everything better. She doesn't see you as a cripple, and you're surprised that there is this kindhearted woman, beautiful inside and out, who loves you unconditionally. You both fall in love and share everything together. Tragedy strikes, as usual, and she is taken by death, and you are, again, left with nothing. You see this repeating pattern in your life, and it seems apparent that life likes to break your heart and toy with you. It's as if it gets a kick out of torturing you. And at night, your mind is persistent, not letting you forget this, highlighting all the injustices that seem to be thrown at you. So, you numb yourself with whatever you can get your hands on, engage in risky behavior, and try to move to Mars. Because why not? There's nothing here for you. You don't care whether you live or die. And so, as a last resort, you visit a psychiatrist to see if you can find the answer you're searching for. How do you cope instead of clinging to the multiple platitudes you hear from family and friends, and the even the optimistic lies you tell yourself? Because if a doc can't help you, then no one can, and if that is true, then there's no other option than to just accept total submersion."

"I had no idea you went through all that trouble in your life. I only remembered what you told me back in med school."

"I didn't want to talk about it. I didn't want to bother you with my sob story."

"It would have helped to talk about it instead of bottling it up. It's never good to hold in all that grief. We need to address those childhood traumas and heal them to liberate the effects, which we'll try today. With that said, this is the plan and direction I'd like us to go in. Firstly, I'd like for you to visit a pain management doctor so we can get that pain under control. That seems be a major factor in the start of the emotional downward spiral. I'd like to also see you twice a week for behavioral cognitive therapy. We need to find a way to channel and express your emotions in a more positive and healthy way. I would have liked to prescribe some SSRIs, but that would require me to use your name to get the medication, and you want this to be anonymous, so the best thing I could advise is supplements." He writes down a list. "But listen here, Michael. If you don't show any signs of improving, I'll have to prescribe the medications, and you'll have to play ball, otherwise I can't see you anymore. Do you agree to this?"

"Sure, Robert. Whatever you see fit in healing me."

"Don't worry, Michael. Everything will be fine. There is nothing to be ashamed of. The age of stigmatization for people with mental illness is long gone. We are going make great strides, you and I. Just trust me. Now let us begin."

The session went better than Michael expected. His mood improved from very shitty to just slightly shitty, still better than the depressive haze that had been looming over him the past few weeks. The neurotransmitters in his brain didn't even have to fire signals to compel him to drink. With a clear head, Michael decided to go to his loft's roof and stargaze through his telescope. This was a hobby that sparked interest in him as a child. He would remember, even before he could afford a telescope, being mesmerized by the night sky, always wondering, during trips into the countryside, where his grandparents lived, how it might be in space. Growing up during the second space revolution and the race for space colonization during the 2040s and onward was an exciting time as more and more rockets went into space by the day. By the time he was in his teens, in the 2060s, private entities and national governments were establishing and laying the foundations of cities on the moon, Mars, and other geostationary commercial outposts between Earth's orbit and the colonies. Michael had particular interest in Mars because, even with the naked eye, he could see the light from Mars subtly grow brighter than the other celestial bodies when he visited his grandparents' rural home. When he was old enough and bought himself a home and car, he purchased his own telescope—not just any telescope but a high power, expensive telescope, worth a month's salary plus some change. At night, he would point it directly at Mars and view the glow the cities gave off from the massive development projects conducted during that time. He was awestruck. It looked just like pictures of Earth's night sky from space, only the surrounding areas had a slight orange hue.

Not drinking, being outside, and focusing my attention on my favorite hobby is a good idea, he thought. It certainly let him take a break from the confined space that was his mind. Dr. Moss's advice was therapeutic, worthy, and on par with any drug a physician could administer. It was liberating, as liberating as a cardiologist relieving a patient of a clogged artery, only that it wasn't a clot preventing his well-being but language, emotion, and memories. Fleeting notions with no mass—the things that had no physical form but seemed to block the dopamine and other chemicals in his mind, causing an ischemia of happiness from circulating around his body. And with the precise selection of words, like the very precise selection of chemicals in medicine, Dr. Moss was able to burst the emotional embolism and provide comfort to Michael. It had been a long time since Michael had felt anything that resembled peace. It felt foreign. Somehow, in this rare moment of peace, anxious thoughts began to surface subtly, trying to tell Michael he was undeserving of peace. Not wanting to ruin the night with overthinking, he shut that thought down before it could grow. He was relieved. Capitalizing on this momentum and not wanting to leave room for his mind to break concentration, he took advantage of this emotional wave of happiness that would carry him to rest. There was no dread about being home alone or preparing for bed. Michael came back inside, entered his room, and began to sleep, this time without abusing any substances or placing two aspirins on his nightstand for the next day's hangover.

Chapter 3

STRIPPED OF DIGNITY

"ALL SET FOR tonight?" Steven asked Michael. They happened to cross paths while on route to their next hospital assignments.

"Yeah, about that, I think I might just stay at home and take it easy, maybe watch the game or just go to bed."

"Wait what? We planned this Wednesday! You agreed you'd come, man. I thought we both agreed that we needed to get you out of the house more."

"I thought about it, and I don't know. We're a little too old to be going to a Halloween party, you know?"

"First, this is not that kind of Halloween party, with dressing up and all that other nonsense. It's just Halloween themed. Second, it's a Lars Bausch party."

"And I care . . . why?"

"He's only one of the biggest billionaire entrepreneurs, venture capitalists, and philanthropists in the country. Big rocket tycoon owns that one giant spaceline and a host of other businesses. He has a strong interest in the latest science and technology—a real cool dude. Anyway, the guy is known to throw legendary parties and donates the proceeds to charity, and we have tickets to go."

"Hmm, sounds expensive."

"They were. Two thousand each. Which is why you're coming

with me. Think of it like this—you get to eat luxurious food, drink the finest exotic beverages, be entertained, and be a morally conscious and upstanding citizen."

"Well, when you put like that, it would be such a travesty to let all that alcohol go to waste. I mean, how irresponsible of us would it be, as globally aware individuals, to not show appreciation to those droids who toil in the vineyards. The oil they sweat with the intention that their harvest be consumed . . ." He sighed. "It would be a slap in the face and a disservice to their programming if we do not partake in the revelry they expected of us," Michael said, and they both laughed.

Steven gave Michael the address, and they agreed to meet downtown at around 8:30 p.m. Michael parted ways with Steven and headed toward the far side of the hospital's north wing. Today was Michael's day to work in the research laboratory. He was tasked with instructing and assisting the new research and hospital residents in their collaborative ongoing experiments in the field of cellular senescence and anti-aging, as well as lead administrator of the project. Forty minutes remained before the close of lab, prompting the students to clean everything in a hurry for the start of their Friday night plans. The sinks went off, the supplies were cleaned, and the experiments were sealed in immaculate containers to avoid tainted and skewed results come Monday morning. Current findings and data were collected in the holographic net drive on campus, backed up for redundancy, and one by one, each scientist signed out and doffed their protective lab attire.

Michael was relieved there was not much administrative work needed. It was as if the work schedule adjusted itself to fit with the night's festivities. Sitting at his desk, he exhaled, and the weight of the workweek faded as he saw the neat, orderly, completeness of no further tasks required of him. The weight of anxiety Michael held when Steven brought up the party earlier that day slowly dissipated as he sat at his desk. The positive mindset he was experiencing post

Dr. Moss's sessions seemed to bring about a series of good times. *The wind and conditions for sail were optimal for traversing new horizons,* he thought, and that new outlook gave Michael the permission to let go and explore anything, allowing for a spontaneous night. He reasoned that the party would be carefree and loose and that he would enjoy himself by matching it.

Michael decided to look neat in his appearance. He gave himself one last look in the bathroom mirror before heading out of his apartment. His body was adorned in an elegant, well-tailored suit that held no wrinkles, an extravagant attire hidden in the far back of his closet that he rarely—and often with distain—would display, not wanting to be pretentious. But, he thought, *I must adhere to the presumed dress code.* Michael's eyes stared at his face in the mirror, making sure he had thoroughly groomed himself. Hair product was applied, covering every twist and turn of Michael's hair, like water flowing through a rapid. Realizing how much attention he put into his looks made him uncomfortable. He felt vain and was convinced that he was a narcissist, but he soon realized that this was the only time he had made a conscious effort to look presentable in over two years. The suit wasn't more ostentatious than what might be present at the event; it was an ordinary, formal suit. And his clean-shaven face and styled hair was not a statement of superiority—but only part of a normal routine he had once done.

Sunset had come, and with the cool temperature, Michael felt a slight shiver, reminding him that it was, indeed, autumn. Leaves were fluttering around, catching Michael's attention as he drove. Observing the whirling, disordered patterns and the leaves coming to a stagnate rest intrigued him. It reminded him of life. Life seemed to oscillate—have its highs and lows. He thought to himself, *Maybe my life's series of progressions is on its way up.* He hoped that he, too, would have rest and order from the chaos of existing. And with that, Michael sped off toward his destination, and the leaves were carried off again by the uncertainty of the wind.

There was a large crowd gathering outside the upscale building when he arrived. Michael pulled into a parking garage across the street to meet up with Steven, avoiding the wait from the valet and crowd.

"Just in time," said Steven. "It doesn't start until nine, but I wanted us to be early cause there's a large line."

"I saw that. Well, with a line that long, I don't know if we'll get inside in thirty minutes. We should have planned to arrive earlier," Michael said.

"It's okay. I bet most of those people don't even have tickets or aren't attendees. They're probably just press and loiterers trying to be around the hype."

"That's a good possibility. Let's go through before my abnormal gait and not them delays us," Michael said, and they both laughed.

Steven and Michael made it inside in less time than expected. While waiting in what they thought was the start of the line, the bouncer at the entrance signaled them. Steven's speculations of the crowd were correct, and they were granted access when they showed the proper admissions. The interior of the nightclub was grand in all facets. From the walls, floors, and ceilings, every dimension was made of the utmost material and covered and layered in finer décor. The main floor was comprised of a large dancehall, a balcony encompassing it, and a bar. Dazzling visuals and light displays were part of the DJ's show. The lower level—which drew in Michael—had a lounge and bar with live music. Michael wanted to go there immediately but was convinced to stay by Steven.

Michael thought to himself, *If I am going to give it a go at dancing and attempt to socialize with any of the faster-paced women on this floor, I'd better get a drink or two to loosen up.* With a drink in one hand and his cane in the other, Michael was engaging in the motions of dancing and struck up small talk with a few women. Across the room, over at the bar, Steven gave gestures of approval and excitement for Michael whenever a woman was closely and sensually dancing with him. When the effects of the alcohol began to subside and the pain in his body started to rise, Michael returned to the bar to get another dose of pain medicine. During a dancing intermission, Michael and Steven began discussing Michael's interactions, ego, and drunk point of view of striking out on getting lucky. After the constant back and forth of trying to convince Michael to stay on the main floor, Michael declared that he was going to the downstairs lounge, claiming his pain wouldn't allow him to keep up any longer.

The ambience downstairs was calm, something that Michael needed to equilibrate. The music and liquor had him smiling and snapping his fingers to the beat. Just across from Michael was a woman glancing at him and ordering another drink at the bar. The two of them periodically stared at one another. She had an open, inviting smile and the seducing gravitational force that lured Michael her way. Michael played many potential icebreakers in his head, trying to figure out which one he would use, indecisive and hesitant, not wanting to screw up his first impression with her. In one continuous movement, he gulped down the remaining gin and rode the momentum it provided, walking toward her confidently, then introduced himself.

"Can I buy you another drink? I see you're quite low there," Michael said. She accepted. "Lovely! The name is Mike." He extended his hand for a proper introduction.

"I'm Nancy," she said, shaking his hand and completing the customary ritual.

"It's a pleasure meeting you, Nancy. Do you mind if I take a seat here? I think that tonight's music would be better enjoyed if I shared the experience in the presence of another."

"Just anyone?"

"Okay, I mean you," Michael said abruptly and smiled. "You don't mind the presence of a total stranger sitting next to you, enjoying this ensemble playing, do you?"

"No, I don't mind. A little company would be fun."

Nancy and Michael seemed to feel comfortable and began hitting it off (though it might have been the alcohol). The conversations were smooth and easy; there was a real harmony between them, finishing each other sentences. They traded life stories and histories and discussed their interests, finding many commonalities. Michael found out that Nancy had a thing for late twentieth-century classic rock music, which was the hook, liner, and sinker for him. Nancy seemed to be developing a fondness for him and gave him a long kiss as the live band started playing slower music. She didn't seem to mind that he could only hold her with one hand at the side of her hip because of his cane. She also mentioned not limiting themselves to only one night, hinting at plans to see him more often. Contentment was a lesser word to describe what Michael was feeling. With all the seemingly great things happening the past few weeks—and his blood alcohol content well over the legal drinking limit—he had transcended and reached a state of bliss, ecstasy, and nirvana by fulfilling his hierarchal needs at that moment. Coming back to his senses, he noticed he had to use the bathroom and parted ways with Nancy, promising to return.

On the way to the restroom, Michael encountered Steven hanging by the corridor that led to the facilities. Steven told Michael that he had grown tired of the scene upstairs and decided to join him downstairs, but when he noticed Michael dancing with a woman, he did not want to interrupt.

"So, you've been here, just stalking, watching us like some sort of creep?" Michael said in a joking manner.

"I'm happy for you, man. From where I was standing, it seems like everything is going well for you. What's her name?"

"Her name is Nancy, and yeah, I think she's pretty great. I definitely would like to see her more, like on a regular basis, you know?"

"I get what you mean."

"Yeah. Well, if you don't mind, I gotta get to the bathroom. Gotta piss like ten minutes ago."

"I'm headed there now—too much food from the bar. I'll join you."

Michael was the first to exit the bathroom. Walking the long stretch down the hallway, he was excited for what was in store for him, expecting a great outcome with Nancy. That grin—large enough to contract the cheek muscles and squint the eyes, the one that comes from being drunk—was engrained on his face since leaving her. Approaching the corner of the hallway, he saw Nancy just outside the women's bathroom speaking with another woman. He could overhear them. At first, he was going to approach her but thought it would be rude to break up the conversation with her friend, so he hid behind the wall to wait. Upon eavesdropping, Michael thought very little of the conversation. He was only looking for the perfect time to say hello, but then he realized they were talking about him.

"Anyway, what are you doing with that guy? He seems like a loser," her friend said.

"He's not a loser. He's a great guy. He's a doctor and has done a lot of work helping sick people. That's very noble of him. Plus, he's cute."

"Yeah, but did you see that thing he walks around with? He walks like he's been hit by a car."

"Don't tease him like that. He's been through a lot and has suffered for the better part of his life and still manages to have a meaningful life. I can see myself having a long and committed relationship with this guy."

"Look, all I'm saying is that you're drunk, Nancy, and your judgment's off."

"No, I'm not. And no, it's not."

"Yes, you are drunk. Look, I'm telling you this because I'm your friend. You're almost thirty-five. You still haven't married, and it's seems like you're desperate, desperate to find love and trying not to be hurt by another asshole, like all the other guys you've failed with, that you're willing to sink this low. He's a cripple, Nancy, a cripple! He's already like that now. Can you imagine when he's older? How much of a burden that is going to be for you? You deserve better. You deserve a real man, one that's strong enough to protect you."

Nancy thought hard about it. But in the end, she was swayed

and decided to succumb to her friend's advice. "What should I do then?" Nancy said.

"Just make up some excuse. Don't worry about him, and don't worry about finding good husband material. I have this great guy that I want you to meet."

"Michael!" Nancy said with a shocked look on her face. She could tell by Michael's face that he heard everything. There was no place to hide, no way for her to pretend it never happened, no way to greet him ignorantly.

As he was making his way past them, Nancy yelled out to apologize to him. He turned around, and they both looked into each other's eyes, silent. She knew there was no way to make it better; speaking would only make it worse. There was only pain in his eyes. Michael finally departed and headed straight home. The only thing on his mind was that he wanted, more than anything, to sleep and forget about the party.

Having already been sedated at the club, and more on his way home, he was almost unconscious. He managed to make his way into his loft and decided to drink some more. As he laid on his bed, almost about to sleep, an old friend came to surprise him. It was despair, and he brought other emotions that beat Michael relentlessly—like a victim being mugged. The thoughts convinced him that he would never be loved and never be good enough. The accumulation of past trauma was resurfacing and started manifesting into real head pain, but the tipping point was what happened to him that night. The lack of dignity and respect from someone he thought he could trust, a person he confided in and was vulnerable with, hurt him—a total disregard of anything that made him human. He only served as an emotional outlet to pass the time until something new caught her attention.

His headache started floating away, as did most of his sensations. His body was finally relaxing, letting go of all control. He could see his field of vision grow dimmer as each minute passed by. Suddenly, he could see the void; there was only darkness. He gulped down the remaining pills of oxycodone he had on his nightstand. As each second passed, drawing closer and closer to his final breath, he thought he could hear and see Katherine in his mind, though he reasoned that it could just be his mind hallucinating, as one does in a near-death experience. He did not mind it, though. If this was his final conscious thought, he couldn't have asked for a more comforting and better one.

Chapter 4

REPRIEVE

"MICHAEL! MICHAEL! CAN you hear me?" a voice said. At first faintly and distant, Michael swore he could hear his name being yelled. Then it sounded fuller. Instantly, his eyes began to focus enough to break up the layers of blurriness shrouding the one calling his name. "You're awake. Good," said a doctor.

Looking at his surroundings, Michael knew he was in a hospital and thought it surprising that he was even alive. He knew without a doubt that he had taken enough to OD.

"Your friend, Steven, found you on the floor. Apparently, you two had just come back from a night out, and you did quite a lot of drinking. He also said you were complaining of pain and must've mistakenly taken more than the prescribed dose. Now, I need to hear it from you. Is that the correct order of events?"

"Yes, Doctor."

"Dr. Acosta. I see here in your records that there's no history of mental illness. Have you been experiencing any depression or had suicidal thoughts?"

"No."

"Alright, I believe you. Your records and demeanor tell me you're not suicidal. Apologies for the personal questions. As you know, being a medical doctor, we must ask these sorts of questions when there are suspicions of a suicide attempt. It's the law."

"Hey, no hard feelings. I'll make sure to have a sober and responsible chaperone watching over me next time I drink, Doc."

"And to prevent you from ingesting any medications while drinking.

"Exactly."

"Looks like you can go. I'll let the staff know you can be discharged. Take care of yourself, Michael. Pleasure meeting you."

Michael shook his hand, and Dr. Mayer parted from the room. Steven was informed that it was okay for him to enter. He closed the door behind him and wiped the fake smile he used to bid the doctor goodbye off his face. Michael waited, preparing for his friend, his friend that was essentially his brother, to address the seriousness of the situation. Pacing around the room, rubbing the back of his head and neck, looking at the floor, Steven thought for a way to break the silence and make sense of everything. From the bed, Michael could see how concerned and worried Steven looked, and it started to make him feel uncomfortable; the silence save for Steven's movements added to the awkwardness.

"If you're going to say something, just say it already!" Michael said.

"You have a lot of nerve, Mike! I should tell them the truth and have your ass locked up in a padded room. You should be thanking me. I lied for you."

"Go ahead and tell them. I don't care. Hell, I didn't even want to wake up."

"Do you have any considerations for the people who care about you? I see my best friend unresponsive next to an empty pill bottle, thinking fast on a clever lie to tell the paramedics. Do you have any idea how hard it was for me to keep my composure while lying to the doctors? I had to let your mother know there was a good chance her son might die. The hell you put your mother and sisters through these past hours, the hell you put me and Gabrielle through—we all thought you were dead!"

"Why'd you tell my mother I was dying?"

"Mike, you were good as dead. I thought it would only be right to let her know."

"Maybe you should have told her only when you knew for sure I was dead."

"Fuck you, Mike," Steven said angrily, headed for the door.

"Okay! Look, I'm sorry for being a huge asshole, and I'm kinda sorta thankful that you lied to keep me from being institutionalized. It's . . . it's just, you don't know how shitty I felt and still feel. You gotta try and understand where I'm coming from, man."

"Apology kinda sorta accepted. All of us are just glad you're alright."

"So, I want to know . . . how did you find me before the OD went past the point of no return? Was it just random luck?"

"Part luck, part deduction. I'll start from the beginning. After I was done using the bathroom, I headed toward where I thought you would be. While looking for you, I saw that woman Nancy, and since I couldn't find you, I went ahead and asked her where you might have been. She seemed down. She was drinking heavily and tearing up at the bar. I really didn't want to bother her, but she was my only clue. She tells me the whole story about you two and that she felt awful about what had happened. I tried calling your phone multiple times, but you never answered. That's when I headed to your place. When I tried opening your door, the chain was on, so I knew you were inside. I didn't want to rush in, thinking the worse, but the worry got the best of me, and I broke the chain since you wouldn't answer the doorbell. That's when I saw you unconscious. I didn't know whether you were dead or not. I couldn't tell if you were breathing. So, I called 911, and the rest is where we are now."

"The paramedics didn't ask about the broken chain?"

"Before they came, I unscrewed the remaining parts and made sure they were in the trash. You're lucky I have a key to your place, otherwise it would have been hard to explain why your door was broken down," Steven said with a brief laugh.

"Thanks, man."

"So, are you going to tell me why you tried to take your own life? I mean, I know you have been depressed for the past two years, and you have had bad bouts before, where you wanted to die, but never to the point where you tried to actually kill yourself. That woman's rejection couldn't have been so devastating to push you over the edge, right?"

"It wasn't just what happened between us, though it was painful. It set off reactions and resurfaced the pain and hurt I thought I had behind me. Memories of sorrow and anguish flooded my mind, and it started to hurt physically. I thought I would never find relief. I was vulnerable. I was so used to shutting myself off from developing feelings for anyone else that when I finally opened up to someone, believing something good could come out of it, I landed on my face, looking like a fool. It made me remember all the times I tried to find a woman, only to realize I wasn't good enough because of my disability. I had reasoned that I would never be good enough.

"The thought of not having a reason to wake up in the morning, other than to mask my pain and broken body with worthless sedatives, and to always have to endure the chronic agony alone . . . it was too much. The warmth and presence of a woman was something unattainable, and it would forever be that way. Those thoughts ran through my mind until killing myself popped up, and it made such a convincing argument. I pictured myself being free from the pain and reunited with Katherine, the only woman who ever loved me. I was just too overwhelmed and downed all the pills, thinking it was enough to kill me, but I guess not."

Steven was speechless after Michael's confession, intending to say something that could patch over the emotional wound and sustain Michael just enough to bring him to a place of hope. But it seemed like an impossible feat. Like a bandage on a fatal wound—futile and in vain. So, he did as any good friend would do and silently offered his support, giving a look of reassurance and trust that everything would be all right. And Michael knew what Steven tried to convey through the silent gesture and thanked him.

Some time had passed, and Michael and Steven left the hospital once he was cleared. They had planned to meet up with Steven's wife, Gabrielle, at Hudson Beach. Steven and Gabrielle wanted to keep Michael's mind occupied and thought nature would offer a therapeutic effect and generate some optimism. Hudson Beach surrounded Crystal City Bay, and the beach's boardwalk had many shops and restaurants, where they stopped and treated Michael to a meal and a few souvenirs. In the later part of the afternoon, they took a boat ride to Accotink Island, a small 2,000 or so square foot island, where they relaxed on the sand to enjoy the mild autumn temperature.

"Here, put some sunscreen on, Mike," Gabrielle said.

"Thanks," he replied. "Oh, and thanks for these trunks. I'll pay you back as soon as I get a chance to sync up with the interface."

"Don't worry about paying us back."

"Well, if you want to make it up to us, you can start by letting us help you get better," Steven interjected. "Or at least try and better yourself in some constructive manner."

"I will," Michael replied. "Watching all these people have fun and enjoy themselves is making me want to take a trip somewhere."

"Good! Take some time off work. Go on vacation. You really owe it to yourself. Where do you plan on going?" Steven asked.

"I was thinking I might go on a road trip across the country, visit the desert or something. Oh, I want to see the West Coast. I've always wanted to visit LA."

"Sounds like a great plan. Gabrielle and I can take off a couple weeks, and we all can go . . ."

"If you don't mind, I was thinking I would just take those cross-country tour buses alone."

"Are you sure?"

"I can handle it. Plus, I can take my time and enjoy all the sights. Those liners are said to have very knowledgeable and thorough tours."

"Alright, well let us know when you decide to go so we can drop you off at the station."

"As soon as I get home, I'm purchasing the first available ticket to California."

"It seems like this beach day has done wonders for you; you're a fast healer."

"Yeah, we're really glad that you're being strong, Mike," Gabrielle said.

"I'm trying, guys."

"We know," they both said.

Sunday evening came. Gabrielle and Steven dropped Michael at the station after spending a day with Michael and his family. To see that he was alright, his mother and siblings threw him a little farewell party. On the bus, the overwhelming feeling after seeing his mother crying started to leave. His mind could breathe a little better after hearing the broken record of clichéd, positive words they said to him. He felt guilty that he didn't want to attend but would've felt worse not giving them a sense of security that he was okay; he felt he owed them that.

The bus driver alerted the passengers that the ride was starting, shouted the first destination, closed the doors, and drove away. Michael drowned out the noise by tuning into his music. Towns and landscapes frequently changed, like a projection of an early twentieth-century movie, looking out the window. With each mile that passed, streams of new and unfamiliar sights entered his field of view; the buildup of excitement from these new places made Michael eagerly anticipate the next destination. The bus stopped at restaurants for dining, introducing various local cuisines and obscure dishes to Michael's palette, food he would have never tried before. At rest stops, he took advantage of the time to explore and survey the land, touching the soil, fully immersing himself in the environment, making sure to leave a presence behind and that the experience of the rural and desolate beauty etched itself into a permanent memory.

Further out west, the bus set aside a two-night stay at the Grand Canyon. During the ride, Michael had made an acquaintance with an elderly woman, Edna, and her grandson, Charles, who agreed to explore the Canyon with him. Michael had never seen this majestic beauty before. At the close of the day, the three headed for the lodge to rest, but Charles pleaded to his grandmother, "Can Michael take me to the lookout points to stargaze?" Edna finally gave him permission, and the two of them headed off. While walking for what seemed to be many hours, drawn by glow sticks shining in the night, they met a family camping at the bottom of the canyon, who invited them to join their bonfire.

The unpolluted night sky hosted the perfect screening for a space enthusiast like Michael. It was not like home, where even if he could see the distant galaxies of deep space, they resembled patches of salt in an infinite black sea. Or as if the Earth were in a bottomless void and the starlight that managed to make its way down was on a wavelength barely preceptive to the human eye. The stars at the Canyon were great in number, so much that they illuminated the ground. With the stargazing he did at home, he could only see through his telescope, but now he could see the whole Milky Way galaxy—with no medium to separate him from the great vastness of space. The moon was not alone but had celestial companions to keep it company during the night. All these thoughts played in Michael's mind, but he was soon jerked from his contemplative trance when Charles reminded him it was almost time to leave.

The next day, Edna, Charles, and Michael were determined to complete the entire tour of the Canyon before their time ran out. Though he enjoyed the second day's tour, Michael was more interested in viewing the stars again. He had spoken with the higher-ups at the park and made a deal, which he paid handsomely for, to borrow one of their high-power telescopes and have rangers escort all three of them to the best lookouts come nighttime.

When morning came and the bus left for Los Angeles, Michael

realized the trip had reinforced a love he knew he had of space. He knew he had a lot of planning to do in the relatively short time before the bus reached downtown LA. There was a conscious effort about the direction he would or should take in his life, and in the end, as he exited the bus, he was fully confident that he had made the right decision. He checked into his reserved room, a hotel near the beach, and once settled in, he made a call to Steven.

"You're doing what?" Steven said over Michael's phone.

"I'll tell you all about it when I fly back east in another week."

"That's insane!" Steven sighed. "You know what? I trust you are making the right choice, and if that will make you happy, you should totally do it. But anyway, you enjoy your time out there. We'll be here if you need anything. See you in a week."

"Will do. See you, brother."

Chapter 5

ONWARD TO THE RED PLANET

MICHAEL ENTERED THROUGH a steel gate. Above, situated in the middle, as part of the gate's design, the frame was fitted with a vectorized swirl pattern with two cherubs placed on opposite sides. The entrance led Michael to a well-kept field, and many bright and colorful flowers laid in selected areas. Stone memorials towered above the flowers, some higher than others. He walked past many grave sites until he finally reached Katherine's. Coming back from California, Michael decided to visit Katherine one last time before he would say goodbye to everyone, starting with her first. He wept as he spoke to her.

"Hi, Katherine," he said, standing in front of her tomb. "It's been a long time since I've come here to visit you. You know I would have visited you more, but I miss you so much already . . . it would hurt me more to see you like this again—it hurts to see you now. But I only thought it would be right to tell you first that I'm leaving Earth and moving to Mars. There were times where I planned on going but never fully committed. But this time, I'm certain. You were the best thing that ever happened to me, and I will never forget you. All those times spent with you made my life worthwhile. Your presence and smile made a cloudy day shine, and you had all the answers that I needed.

"But you're not here anymore, and no, I don't see any reason to stay here any longer. Without you here, this place feels lifeless. So, I'm going on a leap of faith here and hoping that I can start anew and be reborn—my life and mind—on an entirely new place—hopefully a heaven, cause right now, I feel like I'm in hell. And who knows? Maybe the further I am from you, the more I can forget about the hurt of losing you. I will always love you and keep you in my heart wherever I go . . . until the day I die. I love you, Katherine. Goodbye." He hugged her tombstone, left the cemetery, and prepared to say goodbye to his family and friends.

Late in the morning, after leaving the cemetery, the highway and roads were empty. Michael whisked through and made it to Steven and Gabrielle's house in no time. Though he had told Steven about his plans, he was a little anxious; he was about to say goodbye to the only people he knew, minus his family, that genuinely cared and accepted him like family. He didn't want them to feel as though he was abandoning them or that the relationships they made were insignificant and disposable or based on the setting or stage of his life. All he wanted was to say the right words, leaving them with a feeling of gratitude and assurance that they were not a factor in him going away. Quite the opposite, it was because of them, in wanting to make them proud. He wanted to show them that he was willing to try to be strong after his close encounter with death by embarking on a new life journey.

"Come on in," Steven said. Michael greeted him and walked inside, only to be surprised that his mother and sisters were present.

"Mom? I thought I was going to meet you later."

"Steven told us you would be here. Your sisters and I thought it'd be better to come visit you here," Michael's mother said.

"It's good seeing you all here. Hey, Gaby."

After everyone settled in, Michael went into a rant about how he had come to his decision and that he would be leaving the following morning. To his amazement, everyone was understanding and encouraging. There were a few questions about his future plans, as to the safety of space travel and how'd he adjust to the profoundly different environment. He reassured them that he was well-informed and aware of the dangers of travel and reiterated all the statistics and data to prove it was safe to quiet their worry. He informed them that he had a job waiting for him at a hospital, he would be financially secured, and the new position would allow him to be a more active physician, something that would make him happier.

"I'll call you all whenever I get the chance on the ship. And in five months, I'll send pictures of my place—maybe also walk around and take some pictures of Minerva for you guys," he said.

Looking back and seeing his family waning in the distance, Michael, with his luggage trailing through security, gave a final wave goodbye. His mother showed no signs of crying, but he knew deep down she was withholding it, keeping it inward until he got on board or at least out of sight so she could grieve; the thought made him sad and almost shed a tear. Snapping out of it, he stoically showed his ticket and passed through the entrance of the terminal. At the gate, he ceremonially left his visceral belongings behind. Walking down the terminal, he heard the final call to board, reminding him of past times he walked away, but this time, it was different; without a second thought, he would heed to it. He thought this would be his chariot of fire to take him to heaven.

The confines of the ship were massive. Michael thought he and other passengers wouldn't feel trapped in the ample space. The ship was like a cruise liner, where anyone could move around and enjoy themselves. Each passenger had their own living quarters, and if one were to feel the effects of the ship-induced delirium, there was an option to stay in a hibernation chamber. Seeing those hibernation chambers made him wish he had one close by, where he could escape the feelings of isolation and pain he'd suffered. Aware of this, he focused his attention elsewhere before letting thoughts of the past drag him down an all too familiar road.

Instructions were broadcasted over the speakers for the travelers to prepare for takeoff, and everyone took their seats. The ship accelerated, sped down the runway, building up the momentum needed to start a gradual ascent toward the sky. As the slope became steeper, the rockets were deployed, breaking through the Earth's atmosphere. Inside the ship, passengers could feel it rocking violently, but no one, not even the children on board, panicked, as people had accustomed to space travel—some even being regulars. Once out and above the Earth's orbit, the motions of the ship calmed, and the crew set sail on autopilot for the spaceship to reach its course.

Riders kept themselves occupied, seeking out interests that caught their eye. The ship had an array of amenities that catered to anyone's taste. It also had quite a few vices for the more mature riders. From gambling to dancing to a bar that served up choice spirits, those who wanted to get their kicks at their leisure came down to the Captain's Quarters—a popular place for most adults on board. While eyeing the holographic brochure, Michael figured, *What the hell?* and went on down to the bar.

A few hours after takeoff, the captain made an announcement that caught everyone by surprised. He let the passengers know there would be a detour. Apparently, for precautionary measures, the ship had to be inspected at the nearest and earliest stop. The ship would be docked on a lunar colony, where the travelers would wait until the vessel was cleared after a rigorous inspection check. Passengers scrambled around the ship asking personnel for further explanations. The crew and employees reassured everyone that everything was fine, that it was most likely a minor issue, probably the rockets needed to be refueled, but still, they would ask the captain for further information. After the brief period of hysteria, the concerns of the passengers were put to rest when the captain told the passengers the issue. A warning light indicated a slight vulnerability in a part of the ship. There was no cause for concern, as they were only an hour away from the moon, but they didn't know whether the small problem would unravel into something unfixable in deeper space.

The next pit stop would be Mars, five months away. So, in order to avert a potential catastrophe and a mass panic, he planned to inform them partially on the ship, then eventually tell them the gravity of the situation on the moon.

Everyone on board made it safely and walked through the loading dock connecting the ship to the port of Kepler lunar colony. The colony was fitted with many businesses inside its dome, with other auxiliary enterprises scattered around outside the dome. This particular colony mainly served as an intermediary stop for long-distance travelers, hence why the captain stopped the ship to be fixed by the experienced servicemen lodging there. The abundance of lodges and diners also made it convenient for the passengers to comfortably wait until the ship was repaired.

After having checked into an inn and finished drinking a cup of coffee at a café, Michael walked around a square in the city, noticing several individuals offering tours around the crater on their rovers. Curious, he negotiated a deal with one of the men, and after having put on a spacesuit, they headed out of the dome and up to the higher grounds of the crater. Along the way, Michael saw tiny homes on outskirts of the city with fake vegetation outside, resembling lawns in the desert back on Earth, only with gray instead of brown soil. They finally made it up to Kepler peak, the highest point on the crater, where they stopped, as directed by Michael. He wanted to get a great vantage point to see Earth from the moon. When he saw Earth's beauty, he was speechless. The sunlight radiating off the Earth's surface displayed a vibrant blue glow that intensified his feelings of awe.

"Makes you think, huh?" said a passerby.

"It's incredible. I don't think there are words in any language to describe how beautiful it is," Michael replied.

"It puts things into perspective, don't you agree?"

"Yeah, it does. It kinda makes all the politics, hate, and war over minor differences seem silly. What a waste. Up here, you can see there are no borders—that it's all one. And all of it seems like ancient history, but it wasn't that long ago. I'm just glad the world is united now."

"Same here."

"I'm sorry, your name is?"

"Sean. Pleasure to meet you."

"I'm Michael. And likewise."

"So, what brings you all the way out here, far from Earth?"

"Starting a new life on Mars."

"Mars? Pff. That's a long ways out."

"Needed a new surrounding and a different pace. Things just seemed stagnate. So, how about you? You moving, or do you live out here?"

"I'm a local, lived here since '62. I live about a quarter mile from here in a bungalow. I'm a farmer. I work down at the indoor farm going toward the Copernicus colony—real agricultural marvel. Had the day off, so I decided to come out hiking and gaze at the Earth."

"Incredible! Thirty years out here. How long did it take to adjust to this terrain?"

"Not that long. Long as you're active, you'll stay healthy and fit. So, about this Mars business, what's that really all about?"

Michael was hesitant but realized he would never see this man again, and like a sinner confessing his sins to a priest, he went into deep conversation, admitting everything and his motives for leaving. He told him about the hardships, pain, and Katherine—how there were no anchors tying him down, and it was time to move on.

"You gave up so fast. There are plenty of women out there. Someone would have come into your life eventually."

"I don't think so. Women just see me as this crippled man and pay me no mind. Katherine was the only woman who said a romantic word to me. It seems like everywhere I went, I wasn't accepted. I think Katherine was a once-in-a-lifetime thing for me."

"And moving to Mars will change that?"

"No, but maybe in a new world, the odds will be different. Maybe love, adventure, and uncertainty will adjust themselves more favorably to the new odds. And even if there isn't, it sure beats staying back on Earth wondering what if—at least I could say I took a chance and didn't give up so easily."

"I can respect that. Wherever you go, I hope you can always feel like you're home—like you're accepted. That's unfortunate that people treated you harshly back on Earth and all because of a disability. No one should be ostracized like that, especially in an age like this. I would've thought people wouldn't discriminate because of a handicap. Well, I best be going. I need to be getting back home. Again, all the luck to you, Michael. I send you off with agape love—may you find what you seek."

"Thank you. And best wishes to you and your family."

Back alone in the soundless vacuum, Michael thought it'd be a good time to return to the inn. He phoned the tour guide and was picked up in twenty minutes.

Michael checked at the front desk to inquire about the status of the ship. The clerk had just been updated that the ship would not be ready for a while—about an Earth day—and that he would be wise to get comfortable in his room. Though he'd like to keep moving, he didn't mind having to stay on Kepler. He decided to sleep and wait until morning to explore around the dome. When he was finished, he'd reenter the ship's line at the port.

A month into the trip, after leaving Kepler Colony, the passengers seemed to get a bit restless. To gather himself and uplift his mood, Michael would make sure to find an object that would shift his focus from the weariness of space travel. This object grabbed his attention more than any other amusement the ship had to offer. Early in the morning and late in the evening, relative to his schedule, he would roam around the outer frame of the ship. The ring was encapsulated with thick, impenetrable glass and encircled the ship and served as a deck. Being there, looking out in deep space, silent and still, the ambience of the moments he'd spent walking and gazing out into the void of space would calm him.

While basking in the experience of it all, he had the sudden realization that he'd had this exact experience before. *Is this déjà vu?* he thought. Then he realized that he was dreaming. He remembered it clearly. He had indulged in the ship's amenities, grew tired, decided to hibernate, and scheduled to wake one week prior to the estimated landing date. Michael wasn't alone; most other passengers opted to hibernate as well, fearing they'd go insane from the trip. The ship's crew would also hibernate, although only in shifts.

"Welcome back, Mr. Acosta," the automated greeting from the chamber said to Michael. A good fifteen minutes passed before the machine let him out. His vitals were checked—heart rate, blood pressure, oxygen, and even bone and muscle density. The fluid was drained, and he could finally see without distortion. The breathing mask finally stopped as the diagnostics cleared that he was able to sustain himself with no assistance. All the parameters on the displays reset to zero as the machine was ready to house a new soul. Michael was free to go.

Returning to the deck, once he recollected and groomed himself, he could see, not too far in the distance, Mars. This new world now laid within his grasp. It was surreal and felt like a dream seeing this alien world that looked like his distant home; he hoped he wasn't dreaming again. He touched the glass and felt the coldness to make sure. Looking at Mars, ideas flooded his mind, giving him a picture of what his life could have in store for him. Though the thoughts were good, he quickly shut all those expectations down and thought it would be better to let uncertainty lead the way; he did not want to be a control freak like he was on Earth. *Maybe being unconscious and away from my thoughts for almost a month and a half has changed my patterns of thought,* he wondered. He found it liberating, feeling reborn, an appropriate new beginning when entering a new world.

About six days after awakening from his deep sleep, the ship was about ready to enter the Martian atmosphere. All the passengers settled in their seats and braced themselves. This was it; this would now be their home. The ship slowly came to a stop at Minerva Spaceport. Traffic was nonexistent, allowing those on board to ease and flow to disembark the ship. Getting out, Michael found his surroundings a bit of a drab. Besides the abundance of sand, the only evidence of human presence seemed to be the airfield. He was soon taken out of his bleak feelings toward Mars when others started pointing and shouting for him to look in the opposite direction.

In the distance, he could see the skyline of Minerva. The spaceport was a couple miles south of the Valles Marineris River, on which the city was situated on. While being driven by a cab, he slowly started seeing the transition from desolate land to a fertile oasis. Signs of human ingenuity and architecture started appearing in small increments; sparse communities with hamlets, small towns, and then the outskirts of Minerva followed. His cab and others from the spaceport were stuck in gridlock entering the city. From his vantage point, the elevation was high, allowing him to see most of Minerva and into the horizon. The Valles Marineris River flowed to the northeast, and he wondered how long it took man to irrigate the water that flowed all the way down from the Martian poles. The transformation of Mars from nothing to its current state was an amazing accomplishment. How the first colonists developed and terraformed so it could support life was truly spectacular and left Michael with a slight feeling of inspiration. He must have spent fifteen minutes staring into the distance, as the cab was only moving in microscopic units of measurements. He took a final deep inhale of this new Martian air, and traffic started to decongest while exiting the highway ramp into the main avenues of the city.

At 1604 Olympic Drive, Michael was dropped off. This was to be his new address. The building, a condominium complex of about eighteen stories high, laid in the northwest part of Minerva. There were many amenities inside, including a gym, pool, and a basketball court on the roof. Michael knew he'd probably never have time; the functionality for him to use those extra features would be tough, but he found it comforting that staff were available twenty-four hours a day (same as an Earth day). He loved that the condominium was close to public transit, parks, and a variety of essential stores. It was also not far from his workplace, and thinking about his new job, he couldn't have picked a better place to live.

Michael was overcome with a relaxed feeling while looking up at the building. He figured it must've been from the large fountain's constant noise in front of the building. The landscaping induced relaxation and had a quality Michael couldn't figure out, a serene ambience. It felt good. Maybe it was the hypnotic, continuous sound from the water; whatever it was, he'd make sure to get outside often. A few employees greeted Michael with his belongings and escorted him to his new residence. His new room number was two, and he was on the eleventh floor, a bit of a letdown from his Earth home, but at least he had a balcony with a grand view that made up for not having the top floor. Before the staff left, Michael asked them where the sights and spots were to visit; they recommended an endless list.

Walking down the streets and hopping from streetcar to streetcar, Michael decided to case the city, again letting randomness and uncertainty lead the way. While browsing through the windows, he saw a store that caught his attention. There, on display, the most adorable golden retriever puppy sat, staring right at him. Michael knew if he left, he'd probably never see that dog again. So, he adopted him. He purchased a leach and collar embroidered with his given name—Nash. Michael took Nash to a park midway between his house and the dog store, and they played for the rest of the afternoon. When they both were exhausted, they sat down, and Michael petted Nash while reflecting on his day. He liked the uncertainty and spontaneity of the day's events. He knew uncertainty ruled his life, but this time, he didn't let it bog him down or spur up a need to control things; he welcomed it gladly. Letting go felt liberating. He made all the thoughts he had about himself—feeling unworthy and unloved—disappear and felt indifferent to it. He did not know what was in store for him, but it didn't matter; it was nothing to be anxious or afraid about. And while looking at Nash, he had no fear in the world of Mars; he knew that everything was going to be fine.

Chapter 6

MARTIAN MONOTONY

"ALRIGHT THEN. THAT should do it. I think we covered everything. If you get hungry, help yourself to anything that's in the kitchen—well whatever is in there. You'll have to excuse me for not having food. I don't cook. Well, actually, I don't know how, so I just buy my meals."

"Don't worry, Mr. Acosta. I'll be fine."

"Good to hear. Remember, Rachel, in the event of any emergency, give me call, okay?"

"I will, but trust me, I'll take very good care of Nash. Thank you again, Mr. Acosta, for this sitting job. I really need the money for school."

"Not a problem. I'm glad to help. And thank you for agreeing to dog-sit on such short notice. Well, I'm off to work. I should be back here in the evening. Bye."

A week has passed since Michael arrived on Mars. He took the bus and headed uptown to Parson's Memorial Hospital. Michael found public transportation to be much more palatable on Mars. His job and everything he needed were convenient bus rides away. He breathed in the air—not a hint of a repugnant smell. There was no sight of any nefarious characters or any potential pickpocketers. *Nothing like home*, he thought, and in that assurance, he eased up and exhaled—

what a relief to enjoy the rest of his ride and see all the city sights.

Advertisements promoting the latest trends on the markets were strewn everywhere. Apparel, gadgets, services, you name it—it was alluring, achieving their marketing goals flawlessly. Signs advertising living spaces were abundant, too, with cranes and unfinished buildings stacking higher and higher, highlighting the demand that more was needed and were on the way. A little further from Michael's seat, a girl pleaded with her mother to buy a new toy; the mother reassured her with a promise that she would, to which Michael hoped she'd keep it. To his left, the bus route was to pass a restaurant he had quickly grown fond of. It reminded him how much he loved their menu and that he hadn't eaten breakfast. The bus was three blocks from the hospital, and all he wanted was to sneak into the cafeteria before the dean or a chairman of the hospital saw him so he could satiate his need.

Though in pain all the time, being disabled had a few perks; sometimes, although seldomly, people would be generous and give priority to Michael in public settings. It didn't decrease the pain, but it certainly helped. Michael made it to the cafeteria with the help of people on the bus and in the hospital giving him priority in line.

"Michael!" yelled a distant voice.

He hesitated to turn around and respond because he knew who it was. It was the dean of the hospital, Darren Harlow.

"This is a surprise! I thought I'd meet you at the main entrance and was on my way there now," Darren said.

This was an awkward moment for Michael. He wanted to greet his new boss right away and was caught off guard, but he didn't want to start off with an unprofessional impression right off the bat. His mouth was still filled with food. Cane in one hand and breakfast bar in the other, how could he possibly greet him and shake his hand formally without looking like an uncivilized klutz? Thinking fast, he remembered that he had a bottle of water in his backpack. In a swift movement, he placed his bar in his bag, pulled out his water and medication, and took it, buying him time to gather himself.

"One moment," he said while gulping it down. *Phew!* "Apologies. I was eating something to take this with; otherwise, I'll have pain in my gut and joints."

"Oh, it's all right. Take your time."

"It's a pleasure to finally meet you, Mr. Harlow. I can't tell you how much I look forward to working here," he said after tidying up.

"Likewise, Michael. We are glad to have you on board as the new head of our department of internal medicine. We were thrilled when you responded to us. We were beginning to think we wouldn't hear from you because of the long delay—must have been rather busy, I suppose. Come and follow me. I'll introduce you to the board, show you around the hospital and your domain, and give a little overview on what you'll be doing. The rest will be briefed by the staff there."

After the long formal introductions, Michael was ready to become acquainted with his position and responsibilities. He couldn't have gotten out sooner. He had felt like an autonomous greeting machine, stuck in a never-ending groove of forced smiles, handshakes, and flattery but having none of the benefits of being unaware like a robot. Darren handed over the rest of the orientation to a younger physician of the department. He was tasked to get Michael up to speed on the wide spectrum internal medicine covered for the hospital. There was a bit of excitement over the news that he'd regularly visit patients—and not the kind of patients he was used to that could be cured with a child's first aid kit. *Real patients.* A lot of patients he would expect to see would be post-op and other long-term patients. *Finally, I'm needed*, he thought. He was given a change, and this would help him to keep his mind busy. The lab was a great place, but being there drove him mad. It was too quiet—the perfect breeding ground for depressive and loveless thoughts to spawn in his head. And though he was indifferent to those thoughts ever since exiting the hibernation chamber, he did not want to risk its return because of a quiet environment. This new, fast-paced, and hectic environment is what he needed.

To unwind the built-up tension from work and curve the boredom from his open schedule, on his day off the following weekend, he decided to go to the Martian History Museum in Minerva. At the entrance, an inscription was written on a banner underneath a holographic slideshow of important figures of Mars. It read, *"This museum is dedicated to all the men and women who sacrificed and contributed to the birth of this planet."*

Further inward, the museum catalogued and showcased significant available artifacts that laid the foundations of Mars. On display were the first spacecrafts and rovers that successfully landed on Mars from oldest to newest. Though most were recent, some were almost a century old. Their condition appeared to be fair, with only minor damages here and there. In another exhibit, the first shuttle that brought the first human explorers was displayed. To much amazement, the first human expedition to Mars was successful, even in the face of all the critics and naysayers. Michael took the stairs to the opening of the capsule, looked inside, and thought it was very cramped. For a moment, he could get an idea of what it might have felt like for those brave astronauts—*Very rough*.

The next exhibit, which also generated a lot of buzz around the museum, was the to-scale replica of the first permanent habitat a crew used in the early dome colonies. It was fascinating that all the cities on Mars came about from terraformers who lived in humble abodes like the display. A monitor on a counter inside ran a video that showed the daily life of the astronauts. The video chronicled key missions in the transformation of Mars and demonstrated the application of the various tools laid around the exhibit. Also shown in the video was the location of the ruins of the Valles Marenaris Colony. That intrigued Michael, and since the field was a couple miles from Minerva, he thought he'd make a visit there soon.

In the museum's upper floor, a screening for a short film was being held in the museum's theater. Michael thought it looked interesting and figured he'd see it. It also gave him a chance to rest;

his feet ached, and his chronic pain from standing all day fatigued him. The film documented the history of Mars—from ancient civilizations viewing the planet in the night sky on Earth to the first successful flying and rocket aircrafts and the many space missions the people of Earth took to fully colonize Mars. The astronauts and colonizers had courage, recalling the harsh voyage they endured and the will to overcome the natural challenges, disasters, and setbacks on the planet. The great minds that engineered and architected the transformation of Mars were also given spotlight. The film finally ended on the future of space exploration. Government and private entities, with Mars being a starting point for further manned missions to deep space, set out next to colonize Europa, Titan, and beyond. Already in the works were the testing and launch grounds set up in different parts of Mars, with an IASA base not much further south than the spaceport Michael arrived at.

Crews at the IASA base were working diligently. Overlooking the hill, Michael could see the professionals coming in and out of the hanger, knowing they could only be finishing up one thing. The entire base looked ready for launch, and everything seemed completed, but the rocket was still being prepped. At times, it would make an appearance, testing its propulsion. He remembered his first time seeing this place, how empty it was, back when the raw steel laid on the ground and the scaffolding and printing cranes lightly covered up the exposed skeletons of the current buildings. That was two Martian years ago, and now the challenge to establish a waypoint on Titan was about to be taken by IASA. The launch was scheduled for late winter; it would unknowingly be a Christmas gift and an early birthday present for Michael. He was woken up from his exciting daydream of the launch by the timer on his interface; if he was to make it to work on time, he'd better start heading back to the city.

It was a busy day for everyone, not just in internal medicine but for the entire hospital. There had been a shortage of nurses, and many physicians took leave for holiday vacations. To lessen the load, Michael's department took in more of the less serious cases from the emergency room. Since he was not a surgeon, Michael covered more patients and had no breaks at all, except to use the bathroom for exactly two minutes. Michael did not mind, he quite enjoyed it, and the adrenaline rush lessened the pain. What he didn't like was the shortage of nurses to help him when he required an extra set of hands.

"Gloria, I'm going to need a nurse to help me with this one," he said, hoping there was someone available. "Donna! Rita! Is there anyone free to help? Shit!"

Michael had to sew up a deep wound on a thirty-five-year-old male involved in a culinary accident—an experienced chef. The problem was, he needed to set up the machine for the wound to be dressed, but there was no one to apply pressure on his forearm. Thinking quickly, he made a tourniquet from latex gloves and used a combination of teeth and hands to balance with his cane, tying it tight.

"Hold on. This should only take moment. Can you feel anything?" he asked the man.

"No."

"Good, that means the meds are working. Alright, almost done."

The machine sewed it up, and Michael left the man to recover.

"I'm here! I heard you calling for help. You need something?" Gloria asked Michael, winded from the hurry.

"It's fine. I'm already done."

"I'm so sorry."

"No need to apologize. I just hope the hospital can hire some more help soon, or we won't be able to tend to the patients in a reasonable time," he told her.

"Don't worry, Michael. Rumor has it, this coming week, the hospital is bringing in a slew of nurses they've been training."

"Hope so. We have a lot of people to care for, and we owe them the best care we can give. Keeping my fingers crossed. Let's hope they're fast learners."

"You know it!"

"Would you join me to treat this next patient?"

"Sure thing. Glad to help."

Michael let out a big sigh of relief on his terrace, the temperature already at negative six degrees Celsius and dropping. That night, he didn't return home until 9:30 p.m. and had apologized to the dog-sitter for arriving late, offering to pay extra for the inconvenience. He went to the rail's edge and looked down the street, watching the nightlife. It became a regular routine for him. Already exhausted from work, watching people pass by had a hypnotic quality and would send him off to sleep.

He did not care, though. He was happy that he was too tired to think. Back then, he would need to heavily medicate and drink himself to sleep, but that was a thing of the past, quite an accomplishment. Before, he would need to be caught in the middle of a chaotic, drunken, melodramatic creation of his own making to fill the void, but now, he was totally unresponsive, and it was peaceful. His insides were no longer flesh but hollow and tin, devoid of emotion, but this was fine with him; he'd rather feel nothing—avoiding the intense sadness that would cause insomnia. He stuck to the strict routine of taking care of his responsibilities and enjoying a brief recreational period. He had become the unaware robot he wanted to be. And this void gave him equanimity, which produced restful sleep. He breathed in, withdrew from his contemplating, and opened his eyes to see the activity below. There were many people walking the street, as was usual on a Friday night. He found nighttime Minerva to be very interesting and would pick out a person to keep an eye on until they got out of his range. A man walking his dog strutted down Olympic until he made a right at the pharmacy a block down. A group of lively women entered Zack's venue, the place hosting a performance by an up-and-coming band called Burn, and he wondered how the show would be. Down at the corner of Olympic and Audubon, at the plaza, there was a large wait for a new five-star restaurant. Overhead, a plane flew by, its engine noise reverberating loudly, on par with the street sounds. After enough time, he had grown tired and was ready to sleep. The worry of the staff shortage at the hospital left him, and he had faith that, come Monday morning, it would resolve.

Chapter 7

THE ABILITY TO LOVE AGAIN

THERE WAS A knock on his office door late Monday morning. The display clock read 10:59 a.m. Michael was going over patient charts, about ready to head out for lunch. The rumor of more nurses arriving was true, allowing him to finally have a break after two weeks. Again, there was a knock. Figuring it wouldn't stop until he responded, he gave the nameless person permission to come in through the intercom. It was one of the nurse mangers, Beatrice. A patient with a rare form of cancer wanted a doctor's second opinion. This patient's previous doctor's protocol failed, and he even tried a new treatment, but there were no results, and the doctor had nothing further to try.

"No," Michael said after viewing the patient's history and prognosis. "His former doctor is right. There's nothing we can do for him."

"That's what I told him, but he insists on hearing it from you; otherwise, he says there's still a chance. He's seen your credentials and knows you're a renowned doctor."

"First of all, I'm not an oncologist. And second, there is no therapy to treat his aggressive and rare form of lymphoma—even with today's medicine. Now, if he had a more common cancer, he'd be healed—no problem. But this . . ."

"I know you said there's nothing you can do for him, but do you think you could let him know gently? He respects you, so if he hears he's terminal from you, he'll accept it."

Sigh. "Alright, I'll give it to him directly . . . but with compassion. Don't worry."

Mr. Chu was in room 132. He was admitted late the previous night due to complications from his late-stage cancer. The metastatic masses were throwing clots around his body, and one lodged into his lung, causing a pulmonary embolism. The doctors were amazed he made it and more amazed by his current state. Timothy Chu was very emaciated and weak, and the only thing his personal doctor, oncologist, and the hospital could offer was palliative care. But he would not give up easily. He was determined to beat this thing.

"Mr. Timothy Chu. Hi, I'm Doctor Acosta. It's nice to meet you," Michael said as Timothy struggled to greet him.

Michael knew it was going to be tough to crush all his hopes. To his left was Timothy's family—a wife and three children, two boys and one girl, which he greeted as well. On top of that, Mr. Chu was the sweetest and gentlest human being. Even during the pain and agony, he greeted Michael with a genuine smile that could light up the world.

"Can I fix your pillow for you, Mr. Chu?"

"Well, okay. Are you here to discuss the new treatment plan? All the other doctors told me you can't help me, but I know you can," he said as Michael readjusted his pillows.

"There you go. Yes, actually. I would like to discuss treatment. I see that you've had quite the journey, Mr. Chu. Blastic NK-cell lymphoma. Boy, that's no walk in the park, and you've come a long a way. I'm sure Doctor Mendelson will testify that you have been his most resilient patient. And I know that you know the time and dedication scientists and doctors put into finding cures for diseases. The medical field had made great strides. Even ten years ago, someone diagnosed would not make it past five years—but here you are, fifteen years later, still fighting. But it goes without saying, Mr. Chu, that there's only so much we can do for you. In the past, most major cancers were incurable, but now, they're so easy to cure—it's like taking a flu shot. And I know this rare lymphoma will be curable one day, just like most other diseases, but right now, all we have is treatment to slow it down. I'm sorry, Mr. Chu, and to your family, but there is no other option available. The best we can do for you is make you comfortable. You're metastatic, you're throwing clots, and there's no reversal. I'd give you about three days, based on your scans and history and depending on if you clot up again. We need you to sign these forms and give us permission to administer palliative care, or we can arrange for hospice care."

"I'd like to go home and die there," Mr. Chu said after a long delay.

Michael had no words. The room was silent. The only movement was an automatic reaction to hug him and tell him a nurse would be with him shortly.

At the nurses' station, Michael said, "Hey, Beatrice, could you go in and help Mr. Chu and his family get set up with a social worker to arrange hospice care?"

"Actually, Michael, meet our new nurse. Lucy will be taking over and will help Mr. Chu find a case worker to set him up for hospice. Lucy, this is Michael," Beatrice said before leaving.

"Pleasure to meet you, Lucy. You're familiar with our social services department?"

"Sure am."

"Great. I'm going to need you to get in contact with our social worker, Sharon, so she can help Mr. Chu and his family."

"No problem. Hey, are you alright?"

"Yeah. I'm used to it. Thanks again, Lucy."

"You're welcome."

Michael's lunch break would not come. He lost his appetite thinking about Mr. Chu and his family and canceled it. Upset was too light of a word. Skipping lunch, he kept busy, volunteering to see extra patients, logging all data, clearing bureaucratic red tape, and completing all other tasks, but the thought of Mr. Chu still lingered. At home, it was no different. He could not sleep. Though physically exhausted, his mind would not rest. Not even his idle night watch of Minerva helped. He thought of the question the new nurse asked him—was he alright? *No*, he answered to himself.

He's known many terminal patients in his career, but Mr. Chu's case was different. For most of his eighty-six years, he's been fighting to live. Illness after illness, setback after setback, he's recovered, all in vain. This man had a certain quality. Though he could be spiteful, angry, and bitter over his situation, he chose not to. Instead, he persevered. *Who knows how many people this man had inspired? Who knows how many times he'd make people question what they took for granted? Why couldn't this man be afforded the rest of his senescent years disease-free? Was he not more than worthy?*

Michael walked a block down from his condo and bought an over-the-counter sleep aid. Feeling loathsome, he didn't want to make a habit of it and promised that this would be the only time he'd take anything to fall asleep. All that mattered was making it through the night.

At 5 a.m., his alarm went off. Not even dawn, Michael knew it would be a bad day. He could feel debilitating pain, rendering him disabled, even while lying motionless. From his spinal column, spreading out to the large auxiliary limbs, it seemed as though someone wrapped his entire body in a cast of iron and drove eight-inch stakes through his joints to destroy the cartilage keeping him mobile, while inflammation hypersensitized his nerves and caused burning spasms. He was devastated. It has been years since an autoimmune flare-up, and he was not in the mood to tolerate this uninvited guest, as it was time to get ready for work. It took five minutes to rummage through his nightstand and find a bottle of painkillers, and it took thirty-one minutes before any signs of relief. *Shit!* He realized he was behind schedule and would be late for work. He got up in a way that minimized pain when moving—little maneuvers and tricks he learned from past experiences.

The warm water from the shower provided some relief for his

aching body. He did not want to get out, but eventually did, arriving at the hospital close to 8 a.m., just a tad later than expected. There was a sigh of relief when his superiors and coworkers understood his predicament. Most even suggested he take the day off, but Michael needed to be there. Being alone was the last thing he wanted. When his mind was given room to wonder, it turned to relentlessness that could easily prompt his body to release chemicals in response to the stress, creating a potential inflammatory cascade.

He felt awful; besides the systemic joint pain, the disease would tax Michael heavily, draining his energy—malaise is not strong enough a word for the sensation. There were no patient visits; he was in no condition to be active at work. He managed to get through most of his desk jobs and decided to go for a brisk lunch. Michael sat on a bench in the hospital's courtyard. The constant checkups by fellow employees was getting annoying, and he found a perfect spot to get away from their concerns.

"Hi! Can I sit with you?" said a voice to Michael, faced upward, eyes blinded by the sun.

"Who are you?" he asked in a confused gaze, placing his hand over his eyes like a visor.

"It's me, Lucy. We met yesterday. I can't believe you forgot me that fast."

"I apologize. I'm still trying to get my vision back in focus."

"Well, now that you know it's me, do you mind if I sit here?"

"Not at all. Go right ahead."

"Thanks."

Michael was a bit confused as to why anyone would want to sit with him, much less a woman. Usually, everyone ignored him, and if it wasn't for the fact that he was head of internal medicine and writhing in pain, he would most likely be invisible. It was quiet. Michael felt inadequate to start a conversation. Usually, for him, a conversation has no substance, consisting of greetings and an occasional platitude or pleasantry, but the silence was beginning to amplify, making the setting awkward, so he thought about what to say. He wondered why Lucy sat with him instead of at the other available seats. He started to question what her intentions or motives were. *Were they pure or malicious, or was she indifferent? Did she merely pity him?* Before he had the chance to speak, Lucy broke the silence. "Is this where you normally come for lunch?" she asked.

"Pretty much—usually with a meal, but not today. Kinda in a lot of pain. I don't have an appetite, so I'm just enjoying the outside."

"Sorry to hear that."

"I'm used to it. Eventually, it will subside, and I'll be in my normal, tolerable range."

"This is what I wanted to talk to you about, actually. Word has circulated that the boss is in more pain than usual, and I saw you limping more than yesterday. I wanted to see if you were alright and if you wouldn't mind telling me about your issue, with all due respect, of course."

"Sure, why not?" Michael replied. *She pities me*, he reasoned. It was a good thing he didn't build up his hopes that she was after anything beyond curiosity.

Michel briefly mentioned his disease and how it left a trail of destruction on his joints. Time ran out, and though he wanted to continue, he had to head back in.

Before going, she asked him if he came to this spot daily, and he replied yes, to which she said she'd try to come by next time. Michael arrived in his office satisfied. His head was filled with blissful byproducts of social interaction and genuine, meaningful conversation, not the measly deficient conversations he was used to. Even if talking with him was an act of pity, he did not care; that little human contact meant the world to him, and if she did not return again, he was happy to have had that. It was a win-win. Whatever pity-induced guilt that led her to talk with him was atoned; her deed of charity and his primal urge for social inclusiveness met the cosmic quota for decent human behavior.

Hours later, he checked the clock, and like that, it was about time to head home. It was a usual night. He spent time with Nash and did his sleep ritual.

The next day at lunch, the bench was empty. It was a good thing he'd kept no expectations; otherwise, it would have been quite disappointing. But just as Michael was about to accept defeat, there came Lucy.

"Hey! Hope I didn't keep you waiting long," she said, approaching the bench.

"Actually, I just got here."

They shook hands and sat down in unison. She displayed encouraging feedback on his recovery, crossing her fingers, wishing him luck that he'd keep progressing. The conversation was natural. They discussed interests and made small talk, but they found the conversation digressing into more, keeping them entertained, like curious and eager children learning about a cherished subject. It was not forced, and both seemed to feel comfortable. Then work and its fixed schedule jolted them out of their private enclosure, reminding them they were still part of the real world, with real responsibilities to return to.

The next day, Michael was surprised to see Lucy yet again, and every day, for that matter. The more they talked, the more they learned about one another. Michael learned that Lucy was a new nurse, only having graduated from nursing school within the year when she was twenty-four. She was born on Mars from parents who settled when Minerva was in its infancy. Michael was reserved about his past, only disclosing pieces, and vague when she would seek further details about his true reason for moving to Mars. Her persistence paid off; after six weeks of talking, he trusted her enough to finally reveal his true reason for moving. She was speechless. The only response she gave was an embrace and an apology that he had to go through those unfortunate experiences.

It was late in the Mars year, and the new year was at hand. Since Mars was not in sync with the orbit and calendars of Earth, the citizens (if they desired) would celebrate the Earthly holidays coinciding with the seasons of Mars. Since Mars was in the beginning of winter, the tradition from the early colonizers dictated that the new year would be two weeks after the initial start of winter, a familiar equivalent to the December-January transition of the Gregorian calendar back on Earth. Lucy asked Michael the week before Christmas if he would like to join her that Friday at Rodgart's Pass, southeast of Minerva, in the direction of Argyre Planitia, where a light festival was going to be held. He said yes.

Dusk settled down early in the evening, and at 6:25 p.m., the sky was dark, signaling for the city lights to come on. Phobos and Deimos lay draped overhead, casting their radiance, also illuminating this Friday night. Michael stood at Your Transport air-cab in Lyra Square, waiting patiently for Lucy to arrive. He had grown comfortable with Lucy, not feeling nervous or needing to impress her, knowing this relationship was strictly platonic, as far as he could tell.

"Sorry, I was held up by traffic—those darn highways," Lucy said.

He was awestruck when he saw Lucy. She was always attractive in her working attire, but she looked amazing with her hair unhinged, a beautiful red flowing down to her shoulders, enhancing her face. Her skin was fair and peppered with amber freckles, and the blue of her eyes surpassed the blue of the seas. *My, is she lovely*, he thought, then he quickly brushed off any hope that a spark could ignite between them.

"No worries. And it's a good thing these things pilot themselves so we can be as flexible as we want with our schedule. Shall we?"

The air-cab landed them at a fair, where the attractions were set up with several displays. The lights emanating from there were so bright; Michael and Lucy saw the destination several miles before they arrived, building up the anticipation. It was the ultimate winter and Christmas sensory overload. Being surrounded by all these stimuli reminded Michael of the only childhood times that were an escape from the hardships he endured at home. When he was young, he questioned why the holidays would bring out the best in people all around him, even in his father's drunken haze, but as he got older, he realized that question was better left unanswered to the mystery of its magic.

Lucy signaled for Michael to follow her down a fascinating pathway. They walked down an endless aisle of lighted trees and shrubbery that led to an enchanted wonderland where everything was white as snow. Set in the middle was a giant Christmas tree with bright white lights and ornaments, with a castle in the distant background providing a great scenic view.

"Isn't it beautiful?" she asked Michael. He agreed.

Michael found it odd that she'd want to come to a setting that seemed romantic. In fact, all passersby were inseparable, displaying signs of affection, making Lucy and Michael awkwardly stick out like a sore thumb.

"Why don't we head back and check out the other displays? Did you see that crazy Santa workshop setup? Looks pretty interesting," he suggested.

"Actually, if you don't mind, I'd rather we stay here at bit. Do you think we can follow that trail of lights to the lake over there?"

"Alight."

It was starting to get a little uncomfortable for Michael. Approaching the lake, it was silent between them, until Lucy subtly locked hands with Michael. Not knowing what to make of it other than thinking she must've felt cold, Michael went along with it, but he still felt awkward in the lingering silence. They stopped once they came to the lake. It was beautiful. Lights were everywhere, and the two moons reflected off the lake. Artificial fireflies made patterns around the lake, oscillating up and down the grass and water. Lucy turned around, still holding Michael's hand, looking up at him, intently biting her lip. Her eyes reflected everything, like lighthouses, piercing him to his core. He broke the silence. "Are you enjoying tonight?" he asked.

"Yes," she replied, shaking her head. "Are you, Michael?"

"Yes. I'm having a great time."

"I've been meaning to ask you something. What do you think of me?"

"I think you're pretty great. I always have a good time when we hang out."

"Me too. I think you're great. I mean—well—I've been meaning to tell you that I'm in love with you, Michael."

"I love you, too."

"Do you really?"

"Sure."

"Why are you not being serious?"

"What do you mean?"

"You're being sarcastic."

"I thought we were playing around. I didn't know you were being serious."

"Fuck you, Michael!"

"Lucy, wait!" he yelled as she ran away.

Limping as fast as he could, he finally caught up with Lucy near a hedge maze and tried to slowly amend his previous behavior.

"Look. I'm sorry. I apologize. I didn't know you were being serious. Plus, I'm fifty-six and you're twenty-five. I figured you accompanied an old man like me just to be nice," he said.

"It's such a shame."

"What?"

"It's such a shame that you have felt so alone and unloved for most of your life that you find it impossible someone could love you or something good could happen to you. I know you told me everything that you've been through, but I had no idea how much it hurt you, and I can't blame you for how you responded. You've become so cynical and had to build up this hard exterior, giving up all hope and expectation to save yourself from disappointment. You were a victim of chance; it's not your fault. Instead of the world being a friend to you, it shunned you and made you feel like an outcast. All that pain and loneliness... how else were you to respond? Becoming numb and unattached was the only choice they gave you. But I'm here to say that you can love me in return. I won't abandon you, and I will love all your flaws unconditionally. You're special to me, Michael. So, if you feel the same, don't be afraid. But if you feel nothing, I would understand."

Michael let go of all inhibitions and kissed Lucy. The intimate moment did not stop at Rodgart's Pass; it persisted, intensified, and carried into Michael's house. Sewn to each other, heavy in passion, the two struggled to enter the house, fumbling with the keys at the front door. The door slammed against the wall behind them, and articles of clothing, one by one, came off, until they were naked in his bathroom. She was shocked by the sight of surgical scars and deformities on his toes, knees, and legs. Before he could feel shame and regret, she looked him in his eyes with reassurance and began to kiss all his scars away.

As the days and weeks progressed further into their romance, the feelings began to grow between Michael and Lucy. Often, their coworkers would catch them daydreaming, snapping them out of their trance. Suspicions about the two dating were raised and circulated throughout the hospital as Michael and Lucy expressed the same grin and would get defensive when any inquiries were brought up about their change in personalities and mental diversions. Though it could've been their paranoia convincing them that they were being targeted by the hospital staff hell-bent on getting a confession, the two of them decided they would keep their relationship private until the proper time.

"I saw you today," Lucy told Michael. The two had laid on his bed until late in the early morning, staring at the pitch-dark ceiling, talking until they eventually passed out. "You looked so handsome with that shirt and tie I bought for you. Seeing you be in charge and directing the residents . . . *uhhh*, it took every ounce of me not to run to you and kiss you," she said while playing with his hands.

"Hey. Babe," he said in a sleepy voice. "I'm about to fall asleep. If I do while you're still talking, I'm sorry, and I hope you have pleasant dreams."

"What do *you* dream about, Michael?"

He paused to think in his hypnogogic state. "Usually, I dream about nothing. Since I've been here on Mars, up until recently, I haven't dreamed about anything. And for a long time, I found that comforting because I used to have unpleasant dreams, usually about Katherine. They were nothing bad, but they made me feel that she was alive and that I was experiencing another day with her. They weren't unpleasant, I guess, but the feeling after it was gone was unpleasant. But recently, I've been dreaming again. And these dreams have been about you. They seem to be hinting at a potential life and future with you. I see you in the kitchen smiling while you prepare a meal in a place I've never seen. And it's funny because sometimes I feel like I've seen this place and situation before in another dream long before I met you. Maybe I've seen you in my dreams before I even knew you, which I find kind of weird. I'm just trying to remember what that woman from my dreams from long ago looked like to see if she was you. But besides that, I get a little worried because I would dream of potential futures with Katherine as well. I don't want a repeat of what happened to her to happen to you. I couldn't bear to lose you, too."

"Don't you worry, Michael. Overthinking will get you nowhere and make you lose your mind." Just as she was about to continue talking, he began to snore and drifted off to sleep. "Sweet dreams, Michael," she said after kissing him on his forehead.

Chapter 8

EUDAIMONIA

THE TIDE RUSHED in, splashing Michael on the shore of Aurorae. At ease and present, sand clung to his body and went unnoticed. His mind focused on keeping track of the tide's cycle, knowing it would return every ten seconds. He felt like the first lifeforms—aware but not like complex organisms, questioning nothing and giving no consideration to choice, only concerned with making note of its surroundings. He felt like he was part of the beach, unable to tell where the outline of his body and sand separated. He was too happy to ponder anything. Nowadays, he seemed to make light of everything; everything seemed better since Lucy was in his life. Even though it had been a week since their wedding and they were still on their honeymoon, every day of the last year and a half with her seemed to call for a special occasion—finally, life was worthwhile.

The view was too beautiful to leave, and a forceful wave drenched his entire body, shifting him down the shore. He clenched what brittle ground he could grasp, pulling himself back to his previous spot. Across the water from the resort, Lucy and Michael could see a myriad of colorful beachfronts, many occupied with vivacious goers engaging in all sorts of activities. The cities on the archipelagos of Margaritifier were all beach towns, and most buildings of commerce attracted and accommodated tourists with their beautiful and unique design—an unforgettable statement left by the architects.

"Have you reapplied sunscreen?" Lucy said under a shady umbrella. "Wouldn't want you to get sunburn."

"Don't worry. I requested that the hotel's automated assistant spray me every eighty minutes."

"What time is the flight for Mount Sharp?"

"Five in the morning. Don't fret. Our time here is almost done. I know how badly you want to climb the mountains and surf the dunes. You'll get your adrenaline fix soon."

"I love it here. It's just not as exciting as going one-twenty down the dunes. You know how much of a little daredevil I am."

"Don't I know it. Just relax and enjoy doing absolutely nothing."

"Whatever you say, babe."

The next morning, they arrived at Aerolis. They wasted no time and started hiking immediately. Staring at the height, Michael knew he was in for a long expedition and had packed extra pain meds in his knapsack. He rented a caravan robo-mule to ride alongside Lucy as she walked the trails. She was understanding of Michael's need for mechanical help and was not ashamed when onlookers gave critical looks of judgment as to why a healthy-looking man was idly sitting while his wife walked, not knowing his outward appearance was only a mirage, like the desert haze. The two started at the west end of the mountain and planned to hike through the peak, then return on the northeast side toward the Bagnold dunes. It was expected to take two and a half days to reach the top.

Much ground was covered the first day, freeing up time to deviate off course and wander into paths that piqued their interests. After setting up camp, they came across trails, some which lead to striking vistas. The vantage points gave them a second look at the ground they covered. The culmination of various landscapes came together to form a breathtaking panoramic view of jagged hills and rock formations. In the background was the city of Aeorlis. It was peculiar in shape since it was half inside Gale's Creator, the rest stretching past the horizon.

The streets were designed in a grid that resembled a model of curved space-time. They decided to relocate their campground to that very spot. With no obstructions in sight—and the mesa perfectly situated on the mountain like a balcony—they would have the privilege to sleep comfortably under the stars—romantic.

"How are you feeling, babe? Are you having a good time?" Lucy asked Michael.

"Yeah, I'm having a great time."

"Are you in any pain?"

"Earlier, but just a tad. Now . . . I'm feeling better that I'm here holding you, feeling and hearing your heartbeat in this desert silence."

"It beats for you, Michael."

"I know, darling."

They looked upward until, suddenly, in deep pondering, Lucy said, "It's beautiful. Do you think there's anybody else out there. I mean, I know there's Earth, and now we're on Titan, but do you think there's other life besides us?"

"I don't know. I think there could be."

"Do you think we keep expanding because we are desperately trying to find that we're not alone, or is it just for resources?"

"I think both. Why?"

"I think we generally are curious, but to get there, we need the means, and it's the ones with money that can provision and hitch a ride. But I don't think it would be so bad if we were the only intelligent life in the universe. If it turns out we are all just wandering among the stars aimlessly in the dark . . ."

"You sure know how to turn the tone of the conversation dark," he said, and they both laughed. "Long ago, I would've found it bleak, but now, I have you, and I don't think twice about those mysteries of life anymore. My world revolves around you. You are my universe. You bind everything, and everything is how it should be."

Lucy was speechless and started to kiss Michael. Tension and arousal escalated quickly to caressing, and then they began to make love. Above them, the celestial bodies watched, applauding with twinkling light—giving a standing ovation and guarding them throughout the night.

At dawn, the cool desert temperatures faded and were replaced with jolting brightness and heat from the sun. Awake and alert, they decided to start the day by making the best of the unpleasant wake-up call, capitalizing on the time added to their schedule and covering more ground. The day passed, and with Michael and Lucy close to the lodge, she decided to mount up with Michael, and they whizzed by the last stretch of trail to make it before nightfall. They sighed with relief that they had the essential commodities of modern living—most noteworthy, the bathroom fixtures and shelter to protect them from the elements when they entered their room for the night.

The next day, they arose at their leisure, not too late, though barely brushing against the border where sleeping in started. There was a savory aroma coming from the dining hall on the first floor, and though Michael and Lucy were about to leave, they could not resist the alluring aroma of breakfast prepared by the kitchen staff.

Revigorated and full of their meal, they set out to the next stop on their itinerary. They trekked through the remaining mile of the dirt path and reached the zenith of the mountain—and what a sight it was! From the top, they saw the path from start to end, but what really amazed them was the view from the mountain's south end. There, hidden, was an oasis. The late afternoon sun glistened off the lake's water, reflecting a spotlight. Michael and Lucy would have journeyed to the desert paradise, but they needed to move on to the next lodge or they'd run the risk of sleeping outside.

Outside the lodge, there were significantly more guests than the previous inn had. They did not anticipate the dunes being a tourist attraction of this magnitude. Lucy was determined to be one step ahead of the crowd and first down the slopes, stressing that to Michael. Michael suggested they rest so they'd rise before the others.

Towering high above, and at a great distance from the dunes,

Michael could see Lucy strapped to her propelled board, gliding effortlessly through the peaks and lows of the sand. Her movements were natural, analogous to a professional surfer weaving through the ocean waves. To his right, he could see other riders being impressed by Lucy and cheering her on. He was filled with immense pride that the beautiful, agile woman was his wife and concluded he was the luckiest man not just on Mars but in all the cosmos. The next day, the two of them decided to go off-roading, an activity they could both enjoy. At the last second, Lucy hesitated but still encouraged Michael to rent a buggy and have fun. With no plan in mind, he went on a joyride, letting the grains of sand carried by the wind lead the way. Adrenaline built up as he accelerated upward, creating g-force, uneasiness, eliciting the whole spectrum of sensations in his body simultaneously.

At the close of the day, he went back to the lodge to enjoy the rest of the honeymoon before he and Lucy returned home. When morning came, instead of walking down the mountain, they took an air-cab back to Aereolis Airport. In two hours, they would be back in Minerva.

They arrived at the house they bought six months into their relationship. Waiting there was all their comforts still in their proper places, left undisturbed. The house was part of a plan to seal their milestone and solidify the future they knew without a doubt would be spent together. Michael bought a beach house on the shore of the Valles Marineris. Lucy thought it was a bit too much, but Michael thought otherwise; he figured they both deserved only the finest life had to offer.

Slumped in the living room couches, they fell fast asleep after returning from Mount Sharp. The exhaustion from the trip weighed them down too much to reach their beds.

"Wake up. It's time to get ready for work," Michael said to Lucy, who was still in a deep sleep.

After resisting Michael's nudges, she finally responded, "What time is it?"

"Ten after five. We were asleep all day yesterday and forgot to set our alarms. I miraculously woke up early, so we haven't missed work. I'll go get the coffee started."

Lucy headed for their shower. She loved the outdoors, but nothing beat the comfort of being in one's own home. The familiar, cold, metallic floors and high walls brought structure and grounded her. Back in the kitchen, an incoming message to accept a video transmission was displayed on the panel connected to the house's interface. Michael took a look, and it was from Lucy in the master bathroom. He pressed the answer button.

"What are you doing, babe? If you don't hurry, breakfast will get cold, and you'll be late," he said.

"Never mind that. Hey, I've been meaning to tell you something—and I was going to tell you later, but when I didn't ride with you on the dune buggy, I didn't want you to think I was being a downer. During and after my time out on the dunes the other day, an uneasy feeling in my stomach appeared out of nowhere. Then, in the morning, we were supposed to go off-roading. I woke up nauseated and threw up while you were sleeping. I was concerned, so I decided to make an appointment with a ready-clinic that day. The truth is . . ."

"No way. It's not what I think it is, is it?" he said in shock.

"Yep, it sure is. About three weeks now, they told me."

He dropped the utensils in his hands and rushed, limping fast, without his cane, toward the bathroom to embrace her.

"I'm going to be a father!" he shouted. He held her for a couple minutes, discussing the positive impact this was going to have on their lives and making plans for the future.

The next week, on a Thursday afternoon during their lunch break, Lucy and Michael consulted with a fellow physician, a geneticist and family doctor. Though Michael had experience working in gene therapy, he was not licensed to perform it on Mars or on himself.

"Don't worry. I assure you, everything is going to be fine. I will take care of you both every step of the way. As I'm sure you know, Mr. Acosta, since this is really your area of expertise, genetic engineering is highly safe and has been in practice—well, if you're talking about Earth years—almost thirty years. Is that right, Mr. Acosta?" said Dr. Benita Jenkins.

"Yes. I want to thank you again, Dr. Jenkins. We appreciate the assurance," said Michael. "I'm just glad our child won't have any genes that would predispose them to ankylosing spondylitis or any of the other common chronic diseases," he said with a tear in his eye.

"Thank men like yourselves for paving the way so that most illnesses are over and even prevented. Come back here tomorrow at . . . let me see, I can squeeze you in at five. That will let you guys come in after work so you don't have to leave early, and I don't mind staying a little later," Benita said.

"Perfect. And thanks," they both said.

Leaving Dr. Jenkins's office, Michael was overcome with joy. "Just think about it. Our little one will be going about and running, healthy, strong, and pain-free, not thinking twice about if their next step will hurt," he told Lucy. His joy quickly turned into sorrow when he was triggered by past memories of pain.

"I love you, Michael," Lucy said as she saw Michael staring down sullenly. "And even if there was no therapy to rid our child of disease, I would still love it, too."

"I know, but . . . it would be heartbreaking to see our kid grow up with pain and have no power to take it away. I'm beginning to see how my mother must have felt."

"I can't imagine how painful it was for you or your mother, but you going through all that pain made you a strong, resilient person. All those obstacles you overcame only added to your unique character, and it's made you the person I fell in love with."

"You have a point. I never would have met you had I not gone through it all. I love you."

"I love you, too."

"Thank man for science," he said.

Chapter 9

WHEN WORLDS COLLIDE

"PROTESTS CONTINUE AMID talks of interplanetary sanctions against Mars from the United Earth government after Martians urged their leaders to reject resolution 1033. Dissenters argue the new legislation proposed by the Earth leaders is one-sided and would undermine Martian sovereignty and drain resources that rightfully belong to us here at home. And now demonstrations are underway at several major Earthian enterprises and embassies scattered around Mars. We join live at the scene of downtown Minerva to . . ."

Michael turned off the display in their living room before the reporter could utter another word.

"Sorry, hun, I don't want you worrying about anything," Michael said to Lucy.

"Daddy, what's going on?"

"Oh, nothing, David—just some grownups still acting like children who can't get along. Don't you worry, Son. Hey, why don't you go downstairs and start up the interface? What do you want to learn this time?"

"Well, I've learn almost every subject, but the one that interests me the most is astronomy, no, physics—no, wait, both. It's so cool floating around and exploring infinity, but it's also fun playing with matter and learning how things work. Hmmm. I can't decide."

"That's alright, Son. We can do both. It's called astrophysics and material science."

"There's really such a thing?"

"Yes," Michael said with a laugh.

"Okay! I'll go run that program. See you there, Dad," David said as he ran to the basement.

"I'll be there in just a second," he shouted. "Boy, he sure is something, isn't he? He's so eager to learn," he said to Lucy, who was in a chair between the kitchen and living room.

"He is pretty special. He's only seven and already excelling faster than most kids his age. He gets it from you, you know?" she replied.

"I'd like to think he gets it from both of us. I'm proud of him. And it's not just academia. He's good at practically anything—art, music, sports; he's like a mini polymath. Well, my love, I must go. Our son is waiting for me. I'll see you in a while. I love you."

"Love you, too."

Demonstrations protesting the overreaching arm of the Earthly government lingered longer than expected, putting the pressure on Martian officials to not compromise until a fairer agreement was proposed. In the subsequent days, getting around Minerva was about as fluid as sand trickling down a narrow hourglass. Even though the hospital was many blocks away from the epicenter, the traffic originating there went to the adjacent roads and airspace.

"Sorry I'm late. It's mad out there," Michael said coming into work.

"Can't blame ya. Pretty chaotic, and the political leaders are in a stalemate—it seems like it's only going to continue," said a hospital resident.

"Guess all we can do is wait it out. And guess all I can do is leave my house earlier. Anyway, is there anything I need to help with or fill out?"

Michael supervised residents on their rounds. Some of the aspiring physicians were well on their way to being independent and fully practicing after they passed their board exams. The program Michael oversaw was running its course, and his understudies were set to graduate the following week. Reliving the experience, he remembered all the dirty hijinks of his days as an amateur med student, reminding him how different it was now. He thought, *Am I really that old?* He pondered for a moment, but the thought left him when Carolina Gloucester, a 109-year-old patient, complained of chest pains warranting their attention. After several tests and finding nothing, the cause of the compliant appeared when she leaned to her side and released the bit of built-up gas trapped in her abdomen, to which she reported feeling better afterward. Everyone, including Mrs. Gloucester, wept with laughter when the seriousness was lightened up and reduced to a bad gas joke.

Evening came, and though leaving work always made Michael happy, he was dreading the drive back. In the distance, the sun was setting, and the sky was painted a vibrant red, almost too red, even for Mars. Looking again, he could see smoke rising. To find out what was going on, he tuned to the news on his interface. Clashes between Earth migrant workers and protesters ensued. In some areas, violence broke out, and Martians set fire to the mills and factories, chasing out workers, forcing them to retreat to the nearest sanctuary. He could not believe it. The peaceful, beloved planet he'd come to call home was turning itself on its head. *Just find a resolution, goddamn it!* he thought.

Centered on the dining room table, a decadent meal was set. The aroma from it permeated around every square foot of the house and into their nostrils. Though the sights and smells from the roast stimulated two senses, it had the culinary magic to stir up a whole host of bodily reactions, chiefly one's ability to over-salivate. But with the current climate of affairs on Mars, all his senses were oblivious to the lovely meal his beloved made. He was lost in thought. Attempting to stare at the meal on his plate, his attention was constantly averted toward the fiery sky outside the windows of the dining room. Inhaling the meal's aroma was masked by olfactory hallucinations of what the smell of smoke rising into the air outside might have been like. All this uncertainty made Michael concerned for his family, wondering how long it would be before things cleared up. *How would I be able to protect my family, as a disabled man, if things were to get out of hand?* he thought. The reality of something threatening his family never occurred to him; all he's ever known on Mars was peace and plenty. He wondered about the future of their lives. He reconsidered his carefree stance about the world and would make the necessary changes to ensure his family's safety—even if it seemed outlandish. Confronting these questions and topics, he vowed he'd make his family's safety his priority above all else.

Deep in thought, he swore he could hear his son yelling his name from a distance. It kept getting louder, eventually yanking him out from his ruminating.

"Dad?" David said. "I've been calling your name for a while."

"I'm sorry, I spaced out for a second. Daddy has a lot on his mind right now. What were you trying to tell me?"

"I was trying to show you what I made at school today. I'm a beginner, so I'm still learning how to build the simple and older technologies. It's a model of a twenty-first-century Arduino circuit. I could have finished by now, but they let us out early from school. Dad, is everything alright? Things outside seem rather bad."

"Don't worry about that. You and your mom—all of us—are going to be fine. Leave that to me. Now, about that circuit, why don't you show me what you've made so far?"

Michael was impressed when David manipulated a potentiometer via his Arduino model kit and explained in detail all the intricate parts that made the circuit board work and respond to his commands. It was amazing how his son, a child, had a noble reason for learning so much; he wants to *solve all the world's problems one day*. Michael was so proud. He reassured his son that he would and told him to keep on dreaming because mankind needed more dreamers. "Honey," Lucy said, walking into the dining room.

"Yes, dear," Michael replied.

"It's your sister. She needs to talk to you."

"Really? I don't remember hearing the phone ring. When did the phone ring?"

"About five minutes ago. That's why I haven't been at the table."

"I thought you were in the bathroom," he said. "Anywho, tell Maria that we are having dinner, and I'll call her back later."

"Sweetheart, I think you really need to take this call," she said with a serious tone.

Sigh. "Alright, I'll go see what it she wants. 'Scuse me, Son."

"Hello? Maria?" Michael said in his study.

"Hi, Michael."

"What's going on? I'm in the middle of dinner with my family. Can this wait?"

"No. Not really. It's important. It's about Mom."

"What about her? Is there something wrong?"

"She's sick, Michael."

"How sick?"

"She's dying. Her doctor says she's got about a year, maybe less. Michael, I think it would be good if you'd talk with her."

"I will. Is she available to talk now?"

"I'm not with her right now, so I can't pass the phone to her. I think you should come visit her. You never came back after moving. You never showed Mama your wife or her grandson. I think it would be good to give her that before she goes. If you leave now, you could be here in five months—might be enough time to beat her prognosis. It would mean the world to her. That hope would keep her alive."

"Maria, I can't just leave right now. It's not that easy. Plus, I'm very busy at work. Not to mention I'll have to get their approval for a such a long absence. I hope they don't fire me when I ask for a year off to go to Earth."

"I'm sure they'll understand."

"Let's hope so, Sister. I'm going to give Mom a call. Thanks for letting me know."

"You do that."

"Bye, Maria. And send my best to the family."

"Send my regards as well. Bye, Michael."

Michael sat in utter disbelief. The silence added more anxiety inside. Finding his center, he inhaled deeply and ran his hand down his face, almost as if trying to brush off the tension of the news. Feeling tranquil enough, he was ready to call his mother. While waiting for her to answer, he swore to keep his composure and provide her with as much optimism as he could.

"Hello?"

"Hello, Mom," Michael said.

"Miguel, it's nice to hear you. How have you been, *mijo*?"

"I'm good, Mom."

"How is your wife and my grandson? When are you going to bring them over? I want to meet them."

"They're good. And I think sooner than planned."

"Oh, that's wonderful, Son. I can't wait to see them."

"They'll be excited to see you, too. But hey, Mom, listen. How are you? Maria told me you were very ill."

"It's nothing, Son."

"Nothing? She said you're dying, Mama."

"We all have to die at some point. I've lived a long life."

"Mom, that's not the point. This is serious to those of us who love you. You should have told me that your health was failing long ago. I could have made plans to see you."

"What does it matter? You're millions of miles away. I'll be dead by the time you come."

"Don't say that. You gotta be strong, Mom. You still have to see Lucy and David."

"All these years, and you never visited. All these years, and you could have brought them here, Michael, but you didn't. You just left and never looked back. It's hard to know you cared, Michael, when you never showed interest and barely spoke with your family. We did not want to intrude in your new life."

"Please don't say that, Mom. I love all of you. I just got caught up trying to make a new life and was focused on rebuilding all the broken parts of me. I'm sorry, but you knew how miserable I was on Earth. Me leaving and starting a new life didn't mean I stopped loving you guys."

"You don't think we felt bad that we could do nothing for you here? Don't you think we felt bad that you left? I was so sad to see my only son leaving, not knowing if I would see him again. When we sent you off, we were encouraging, but deep down, nobody wanted to see you go. I wish you'd never moved. You've missed so much, and there are moments that will be forever unshared between you and your family."

"I know, Mom, and it hurts to know that. I should have made time for you guys years ago, but I cannot change the past. What I can do is try to make it right in this moment and make up for it. I don't want you to feel as if I was avoiding you. I just figured there would always be time. And since I—we—have time, I will hop on the earliest flight possible and come to see you. You can make it through, Mom. I know you can. Just wait a little longer, okay, Mom?"

"Okay, Son. I will. Please hurry. I'll try my best to hold out for as long I can so I can spend some time with my grandson and daughter-in-law."

Michael had a slight smile and relief on his face when he said, "I know you're going to love them. They have been eagerly waiting to meet you."

They spoke for another ten minutes before hanging up. Hearing his mother sound so sick was heartbreaking and upsetting. He could feel how sick she was, the tone and breath of her voice indicative of a malady, death its only outcome. Off the phone, the fortified composure he built shattered like a glass house. His tears came out in spurts; soon, he gave way, and tears gushed down the sides of his face. He placed his head on his desk and covered it with his arms and hands. When Lucy came to check on him, she could see him silently crying, breathing in deeply, then trembling. She comforted him, held him.

"Honey, if I asked you and David to fly to Earth, would you go?" he asked Lucy.

"Not without you."

"I will join you later. I just have something I need to take care of at work. Please, I need you to go on ahead. Can you do this for me? I promise you, I will be right behind you," he said, embracing her face with his hands. She was reluctant but agreed.

"Okay, I will, baby," she said, weeping.

"Thank you, babe."

Late into the night, while David and Lucy slept, Michael bought the tickets for the earliest flight to Crystal City. They were to leave the next evening. Lying to David as to why he and his mother were leaving suddenly for Earth without Daddy was a lot easier than lying about the interruption that happened at dinner. All inquiries of the unusual behavior his father was displaying went away when the prospect of having fun was mentioned. Excitement for this spontaneous vacation drove him to bed early, "So the date would arrive faster," as he put it. Michael's troubled mind wouldn't allow him to sleep, and as he was on the verge, it was already time for his day to begin.

Exhausted, depressed, in pain, and almost entering a nervous breakdown, Michael came back home from work, picked up his family, luggage and all, and headed to the spaceport south of Minerva. Protesting only got worse as they flew opposite the city; the fervor could be felt even further down the southbound ramp, half a mile away and onward. The scene dramatically changed as they drove toward the spaceport. Upon boarding, the family was warned about the elevated delays in spacefare traffic due to the social upheaval and that there might be slight inconveniences of schedules from the resulting chaos. Michael reassured them that everything would be fine.

"So, you'll join us in a week?" Lucy asked Michael.

"Yes, I'll be about a week's time or more behind you guys. My superiors gave the go-ahead, and as soon as the residents are ready to graduate, I'll drive here and board my flight. Son, take care of your mother for me, will ya?" he said to David.

"I will, Dad."

"That's my son."

Sending off his family left a bitter and aching feeling inside Michael. He'd never been away from them longer than work hours, and now they were going to be in deep space, separated by the length of an infinitely wide chasm. The words his mother said to him echoed in the back of his mind, and he could empathize with the feelings she must have felt.

The date for his departure couldn't have arrived faster. With two days remaining, Michael was coasting through work. He was missing his family deeply, and he hadn't spoken with them in two nights. His wife warned him that the communication would be cut off by the spaceline company due to the mandatory ordinance, essentially forcing passengers to hibernate because of supply shortages. Hanging up after hearing her say they would not speak until they were both on Earth was difficult, and it took every ounce of willpower to say goodbye. He made every conscious effort to not look at the clock, hoping the pace of events leading up to his flight would not slow. *Boy, what I'd give right now to be in hibernation, ignorant that I am months away from my family*, he thought.

Inside his office, Michael went over a few matters with a resident so they would have the necessary credentials to graduate. Before entering his office, guests were asked to leave all distractions at the door and shut off all personal electronic devices. While diligently reading, something from outside seemed to capture Michael's attention. At first, the sounds were minor, but they began to pick up. The walls were several feet thick, and the door and furniture were solid metal alloy, making the office soundproof. He wondered how in the hell sound could seep in. There was a large bang at the door.

"Come in," Michael said over the intercom.

Another doctor in internal medicine came barging in, out of breath, wheezing, with a look of shock. He said, "Sir, have you checked the news?"

"No. I don't pay attention to any of it. As of late, it's been rather dreary. And there's no electronic devices allowed in here except the lights and hologram connected to hospital network resources. Why do you ask?"

"Don't you hear the commotion outside? The whole planet is in a state of emergency, and people are scrambling for safety!" Before anyone said another word, Michael and the resident turned on their interfaces and were immediately informed of the situation. The headline read, "Breaking News, Disgruntled Earth Workers Headed Home Hijack Space Shuttle and Take Artificial Magnetosphere Hostage." The motive for the incident was political in nature, urging that the Martian government give way to resolution 1033, thus securing and ensuring jobs for Earth migrant workers.

"Unbelievable!" said the resident.

Michael collapsed on his chair. For a second, he seemed in shock, and any automatic reaction to the news was snuffed by it. The resident wasted no time in gathering his belongings, shooting out the door, and leaving everything.

"Michael?" his colleague asked. "Are you all right?"

"My family was on a rocket headed to Earth."

"Oh—I'm sorry to hear that, Mr. Acosta."

"I've got to find out if it was their shuttle that was hijacked."

"You look like you're in shock. Sit tight. I'll find out for you. What was the flight number? Do you remember?"

"Flight 2104. 2104 to Crystal City."

"Alright, I'll be back. Let me make a quick call. Just hang tight."

Hang tight? I have no choice, he thought. His whole body was paralyzed, crushed with the very real possibility that his family was in serious danger. Powerlessness was too small a feeling to describe what he was going through. Even if he could scream and shout and use every measure of strength, there would be no way to get to his family. Hell, the terms and circumstances left no place for him to start, and it would be futile to exhaust any energy on devising a plan to save them. Just as despair was about to overshadow him, his colleague walked in, this time with a sliver of good news amid the chaos.

"Michael?"

"Yes?"

"It's good news! Your family is fine. The shuttle that was hijacked was flight 6371."

Phew. "I almost lost myself right there. Thank you," he said, looking upward, repeating his gratitude over and over.

"Sorry to be a downer, but it's still quite early to celebrate, sir. We still have the hostage situation going on the magnetosphere; they disable it, this planet is cooked."

"You're right. Go home, Bernard. Get your family, and seek shelter now. And relay the same message to everyone still here!" he shouted as Bernard ran out.

What do I do now? he thought. He was joyous that his family was out of harm's way, but he needed to think of a plan fast. His message to Bernard to seek shelter was an encouraging attempt to boost his morale, but Michael knew it was going to be difficult to find an underground shelter. Every location was bound to have hordes of people fighting their way in for protection; he would be dead waiting in line. The thought of going home and barricading himself in his basement crossed his mind, but it was plausible the local government would issue martial law, in which case he would be unavailable to reach the spaceport for his flight after bunkering. It seemed the most logical and insanely dangerous course of action was to set up camp at the spaceport and hold out for another two days. If nothing prevented him from entering the gates, he would sign over his life's earnings to purchase the first flight out of Mars.

He drove fast through the roads in the vicinity of Parson's Memorial, with the alertness and precision of a skilled pilot, making it onto the freeway ramp in no time. Up ahead, the traffic backed for miles, and he veered off the main highway, onto restricted airspace, running the risk of air traffic authorities pursuing him. Soaring over the barren land, going triple the speed limit, Michael kept a steady hand on the controls despite the car violently shaking. He was moving so fast that the center range of his vision became bleary. His environment was one large, blurred image, but he could still distinguish the familiarities of the landscape, now an undefined assortment of shapes, and knew that he was close. The spaceport slowly appeared, bit by bit, with each passing yard. "There it is!" he said, not knowing his momentous arrival would be meet with an impeding halt.

Encircled around the spaceport, a military perimeter was set up, and it looked as if nothing was going in or out. Michael slowed down, pulled up as close as he could to the soldiers, exited his vehicle, and walked up to them.

"Sir! I'm going to ask you to not come any closer, turn around, and get in line around the other end of this perimeter."

"I really need to board the next Earthbound flight. It's important," Michael said.

"Yeah, so does everyone else in line."

"I've got a ticket for a flight that takes off in less than two days," he said, pulling it out.

"That flight's canceled, and all other flights until further notice. With the hijacking of the shuttle and magnetosphere, it's been deemed unsafe to travel by the Martian government, and it's going to be awhile before anything starts to take off again."

"My family is headed for Earth. I promised I would be right behind them."

"Sir, I'm sorry to hear that, but there's nothing I can do. We are all in a panic, and all our lives are hanging in the balance of some lowlifes, and there's nothing to do but hope—hope that those bastards turn themselves in soon so we can get on with our lives. Until then—and I know it hurts, but you're going to have to cooperate with us, Mr . . ."

"Acosta."

"Mr. Acosta. Please, if you would?" he asked not as a plea but as an empathetic gesture to show he understood Michael's plight.

Michael complied, seeing it futile to go against an army. Waiting it out had the slight chance he could see his family again, but attempting to break in the spaceport would mean immediate death, so he chose the odds of the former for rationality's sake. And even if he managed to get in, with a lame leg and all, there was no leverage he could use to threaten a pilot to fly him neither, and he couldn't fly the ship himself. For his cooperation, he was able to sit with his newfound acquaintance, the soldier, rather than be in the midst of the throng. Powerlessness swept over him again, but this time, it was not overwhelming. What was once an isolated feeling was now a collective one—everyone sharing the burden—and it made Michael feel better to not face tragedy alone. He understood why people would gather during times of trouble, why everyone put aside their differences. *It was comforting, essential, and an emergent phenomenon built into the hearts of every human being*, he thought. And to go at it alone would be too heavy to bear, crushing one's spirit—killing hope.

A certain stillness, peculiar in nature, seemed to radiate from every direction around the spaceport, and the air had a quality of barrenness. Deserts tend to possess familiar properties but not the terrain around Minerva Spaceport; it was livelier than most deserts. The chatter and noise of man and their devices seemed to be heard nowhere. In fact, there seemed to be no one around—nothing at all. Every direction he looked was empty, the spaceport was gone, and familiar landscapes were not in their proper place. A sandy void was all that laid before him. Then, suddenly, after several turns, searching again and again, a great and terrifying sound came from the sky above him. He looked up and saw in the day sky the explosion of the magnetosphere, resembling the death of a distant star. Following the flash, in the distance, Michael watched in horror as the oscillating solar winds began approaching, picking up speed. With nowhere to run or hide, the excessive heat and radiation began to break down every atom in Michael's body, slowly disintegrating him and everything around him. While yelling out in pain, Michael was suddenly jolted out of his nightmare, gasping for air and covered in sweat. Relieved for one moment, he began to panic when he didn't hear or see anyone around him. As he was getting up from the sleeping bag provided to him, the sounds of cheers started to be heard. Michael knew it could mean only one thing, so he turned on the news on his interface and watched with a large smile on his face.

"After almost four days in a standoff with Martian and interplanetary authorities, the captors surrendered, putting an end to the hostage crisis. Officials say there is still an ongoing investigation in the search for other possible conspirators and a hunt to capture the ringleader of the whole operation. . . . Oh, I'm sorry. I'm getting word that breaking news is coming in right now. We would like to bring you live images of the hostages being released and boarding a liner that will take them to be evaluated at Parson's Memorial, in downtown Minerva, where they will be treated for any injuries they may have obtained . . ."

After turning off the news, Michael immediately went to speak with his corporal acquaintance to inquire if word reached him regarding travel. The soldier told Michael it would take some time but not to worry, estimating that it was going to be a week before planes and rockets were back in the air.

Now all Michael could do was wait. He went home, resumed his routine, and reported for work. His flight to leave Mars came sooner than his students' graduation, but there were no conflicts, as all his duties were fulfilled, requiring nothing further from him for the semester. His staff and colleagues wished him well on his trip, and he left his understudies with sagacious words of encouragement, hoping it would ensure their success in the medical field.

Sitting in his seat felt surreal. The very notion that his body was on a shuttle preparing to take off was unheard of a few days ago; in fact, even life itself was speculative, but here he was, along with others, putting it behind them as if nothing ever happened. Already, a compromise had been made by Earth and Mars, where, unfortunately, Mars received the shorter end of the deal. Even though the hijackers surrendered, their goal for an agreement was accomplished. He wondered, *Who was the real victor? It's a shame that it took the threat of violence for political rivals to diligently work on a resolution.* Just as he was thinking about how quickly it seemed society had moved on, it was time to launch. Liftoff was successful, and according to Michael, the spaceline must've been equipped with the finest quality seats; the process was smoother and more pleasant than his previous experience. A couple days in, a news update was broadcasted throughout the enter solar system. Watching on a display in his room, more information was revealed about the hostage crisis, and a big arrest was made.

"Fifty-two-year-old precious metal industrialist JD O'Neil is among other high-ranking business tycoons arrested and charged with conspiracy to commit various crimes, some of which include, kidnapping, terrorism, attempted genocide, and a host of other serious crimes, in connection with May's hostage crisis, when a group of men, former employees of these businessmen, were ordered to hold Mars as ransom of their behalf. Loss of profits due to sanctions and protests drove . . ."

After finding out the motive, Michael was glad his family was unaware of what was going on. He was especially glad David was not witnessing this. It would have been hard to explain that such a petty reason—greed—almost killed his father and everyone on Mars and the population was used as collateral by a few elite men, like some sort of cosmic game of chicken. He hoped that, by the time he set foot on Earth, this tragedy was nothing but a faint memory, replaced by an unimportant, dull headline about a new sensational trend.

After making a call from his ship to his sister's house, where Lucy and David were staying, Michael arrived at Landmark Town Square in Crystal City to meet them as planned, one week before he arrived on Earth. The plaza was a place Michael would frequent in times past, and it felt like neutral ground to keep David away from the spaceport and in the dark about the social climate and anxieties still lingering in the public six months after the crisis. With the bustling going around, David's mind would be diverted from the melancholy surrounding the impending death of his grandmother. The rendezvous had the added benefit of time for Michael to delay seeing his mother. Seeing the public square from a distance, he saw how little things changed. Everything was the same. Atop the stairs, the view above the plaza stores was not blocked. This was a favorite spot of his. It gave a great vantage point of the many structures close and far. The Turnpike Bridge, the Regal Towers, and the tiers of the skyscrapers and their depth of scale and spatial dimensions—it was all there, and he was glad no new structures hindered it. Looking for his family, he started leftmost at a shoe store, then the large fountain at the center, then ending at a clothing store on the far right, before rechecking, this time squinting, hoping to pick up something he missed. Getting a second look, he was able to zero in on his family, who were on the far right. David and Lucy were playing on a spray pool near a trail bordering the Grange River. Walking toward them, his perspective was like a theatrical shot focusing on the subjects, ignoring everybody else. He could see how happy his family was, laughing and dodging the water. It looked like the perfect scene; to an audience, it would seem complete, but Michael knew what was missing—him—and he was glad he wasn't just a spectator watching from behind a screen—he was part of the movie.

"Daddy!" David yelled as he saw his father approaching. He ran and hugged him.

"I've missed you, Son."

"I've missed you, too, Daddy!"

Holding David the best he could, he pivoted to Lucy, gave her a kiss, and asked how she was. She told Michael she and David were fine, her tone calm but her eyes reflecting anything but calmness. "Thanks, Lucy," he replied, nodding his head, knowing she was holding in many emotions for David's sake. "Son, why don't you play right here and give Mom and I a few minutes to talk? If you behave well, Dad will buy you ice cream. Is that okay with you?"

"Okay, Mommy and Daddy, talk as long as you want," David said while playing.

"Does he have any idea what happened?" Michael asked Lucy.

"Not at all. He has an idea that something big happened everywhere, but I think he's just too young to understand the gravity of it or what you were involved in. Same with your mother. He knows she's sick, but he's clueless to the extent of it."

"That's good. We'll cross that bridge eventually, but for now, let's hope it stays this way for a long time. Thank you again, honey, for being strong for him and distracting him while I've been gone. I should have quit my job and gone with you both the same day. I could had avoided such a potential disaster."

"It's okay, Michael. You didn't know it was going to escalate the way it did. Even though all of it unfolded and passed while I was unconscious, when I found out about it on Earth, I was still worried sick about you. I felt like you had died and were brought back to me, and I was so thankful you were alive, and I was going to see you in a month. You're here, and you're okay, and I couldn't be more than relieved. I love you, Michael."

He repeated those same three words, and they held each other tightly for several minutes. As it seemed, all cares and worries did not exist, but Michael was pulled out of the ethereal connection to his wife when she brought up his need to visit his mother.

"I know, I know. We will go see her. No need to hasten things. I just—I'm still trying to brace myself. It's been months, but for me, all this seems like yesterday, and it's a lot to absorb."

"You'll be fine, Michael."

"I don't think I will. I think I'll lose it when I see her all sick on her bed. I don't think I can handle seeing my mother dying."

"I'm sorry, Michael. I wish there was something I could do to help. You don't have to worry about going through it alone. Your family will be there, and I will be by your side for support. If you need to cry, cry. It's your mother. I know I cried when my father died."

"Alright," he said with his slightly wet eyes. "We'll go after I buy David ice cream."

Michael thought about the common saying, "A parent should not have to bury their child," a maxim he felt was far from the truth in his circumstance. Without proof and devoid of competition, he felt he was sadder to bury his mother than she would have been burying him. Michael stood in front of her gravesite, slumped to his right side, supported by his cane, staring at her tombstone. His face was expressionless, and though it was a very chilly day in late October, his callous and detached body did not allow him to react. No shivering or chattering from the wind, he just stood there, in disbelief. Her tombstone read, Reina Acosta, 1999-2104, Loving Mother, Sister, and Child of God, Gone But Not Forgotten. The tombstone was cladded in marble, and the design had a dove centered over her name, with a wreath embroidery underneath it. He sighed, still in disbelief that she was gone. She was so lively those last few days, doing whatever she could to be engaged with the family. To the best of her ability, she rose in pain to play with David and embraced all three of them, despite them insisting she rest. He was happy she was able to see her son, grandson, and daughter-in-law. She had died a few days after Michael arrived on Earth, and though a week had passed since her death, Michael came to visit her every day.

Lucy was speechless behind Michael. She tried to offer comforting sentiments, but there was nothing. She placed her arms around him, offering her body's warmth as shelter.

"I'll eventually be okay," he said, grabbing her hand to kiss it. "Lucy?" he asked.

"Yes?"

"I'm ready to leave."

"Okay, we'll go, honey."

"But..."

"Yes?"

"Let's not walk the same way back," he said, pointing to their left.

"Why not? We've walked the same path every day."

"Lucy, please don't be upset."

"Why would I be upset?"

"Because. Because every day, we walk past Katherine's grave, and every time I see it, it stirs up unwanted feelings I thought had long since gone. That combined with the death of my mother is just too overwhelming, and today is the last day we're here on Earth, and I don't want the memory of her to take a ride back with me. When I left for Mars the first time, I was closing the chapter of my life with her, and I'd like to keep it that way."

"I understand, Michael," she replied. "Do you still love her?" she said bluntly.

Michael was unable to answer the question for some time. Then he responded, "Yes. There will always be a part of her inside me, and there's nothing I can do to get rid of it. But I love you, Lucy, and it's with the same kind of love that I gave Katherine. It's the kind of love that goes beyond the grave and will never die, so long as I'm alive and have breath in me. I also cannot say I love you more than I loved her or vice versa because, when she was alive, I loved her with the same intensity that I love you currently. Asking me which one I loved the most would be like asking a parent which child they love most—they cannot answer because they love them equally, and it is the same for me. If I met you first and became a widow and remarried, that love for you would not diminish or be replaced because of someone new. I guess what I'm trying to say, Lucy, is that I love you, and I need you to understand I cannot go that way again. I cannot look back at an old life—not without the risk of resurrecting it. And this is why I need you to do this for me."

"Okay, Michael. I understand," she replied with a heartfelt look. "Let's go around." She caressed his face and grabbed his hand so he would lead the way.

Michael and Lucy met Steven and Gabrielle at a restaurant in Rowan Beach, where they were taking care of David. They kept David occupied and distracted after the gloomy scene surrounding the funeral, showing him the sights and scenes of Crystal City.

"I'm gonna miss you guys," Steven said to everyone. "You can't stay longer? You just arrived, and who knows how long it will be until I see you all again?"

"We'll try to come back in a few years," Michael replied. "Or . . . why don't I fly you guys out instead, so that way, I don't miss work for a year again?" He laughed.

"Sounds like a plan. I'll take you up on that, but don't flake on us, Mike."

"I won't. If you both are really serious, I will buy the tickets. Don't you worry," Michael said, reassuring him with a handshake.

"Dad?" David said while finishing his drink.

"Yes, Son?"

"I'm going to miss this place."

"It's okay. We will come back to visit again. It will be some time because of how far it is, but don't worry. Your daddy will make sure you come back."

"Really?"

"Yes, Son."

"I want to come back here and learn when I'm older. It seems like there's a lot of things that still need to be solved here."

"What do you mean?"

"It's like a beautiful toy, Dad, but there's parts that need fixing. Remember a long time ago, I said I wanted to help the world?"

"Yes, I do."

"Well, I didn't really think this was part of Mars because it was so far away, but now that I've been here, it's the same, Dad, and that means it's a part of the world—our world. So, I have to help solve the problems here too, Daddy."

Michael questioned whether his son knew more than he was willing to say. *Could he really have an idea of the magnitude of what was happening? And if that was true and he did, how much and to what extent did he know?* He saw the look in his son's eyes. They were piercing and still. They had the look that said, *He knew everything but was unwilling to disclose anything for my sake.*

"Well then, we better start saving up for room and board." He laughed.

Chapter 10

LOVE IN OUR GOLDEN YEARS

SITUATED IN THE backyard of the Acosta residence, a large palm tree, towering several feet in the air, stood adjacent to Michael and Lucy's bedroom, its leaves touching the windowsill. A little bird perched its legs on a sturdy stem and tweeted away, signing a tune. With the sun still low in the morning sky, the rays began to penetrate through the half-open blinds and curtains, slowly revealing an image Michael saw on the opposite wall of their bed. When enough light made its way through, a complete silhouette of the bird and leaves was projected between the stripes of the blinds. The angle of the sun made it so that photons of light bounced off the glass to produce a rainbow on the wall, intersecting through the stripes and bird. Michael found it quite amusing, waking to an unexpected performance of serendipity.

Coming in from the hallway, Lucy saw Michael staring off, smiling at the wall with a droll look on his face. Lucy let out a giggle.

"Why are you smiling so silly at the wall like that?" she said, sauntering into the room and heading toward the bathroom.

Just as he was about to answer, the bird fluttered away, and the rainbow was gone, leaving only stark parallel lines, unamusing, too late to show her the source that brought about her inquiry. "It's another day I woke up with you, the love of my life," he said. The suaveness prompted an immediate response from Lucy, gesticulating loving and adoring faces while she brushed her teeth.

Michael decided it was time to start his day, and he mustered up the strength, breaking through the threshold of laziness keeping him on his bed, swiveled his creaky body, and planted his feet on the floor, springing himself up to stand and stretch. As Lucy finished brushing, she came out of the bathroom and reminded Michael to hurry.

"Alright, give me a couple more minutes to stretch. I'm trying to get this joint in my lower lumbar to crack, and if I don't, I'm going be uneasy all day," he said while stretching.

"Need I remind you David will be here in about forty-five minutes?"

"I know. Don't worry. I'll be ready by then."

"It's been fifteen years since he's been gone. Let's try to welcome him on schedule."

"I know, honey. I'll be downstairs, waiting in the foyer with excitement, just like you," he said, staring at her.

After giving her a kiss, they parted ways—Lucy downstairs to prepare and arrange some last measures of the planned gathering and Michael into the bathroom. Like with every morning, he started his day hobbling over to the counter, taking his daily regimen of pills and gulping them with sink water clasped in his hands. In the span of fifteen years, he'd noticed how seasoned his face had become. His hair had become a palette of salt and pepper, and his face had become slightly withered and cracked, like the desert sands of Mars. He figured the anti-aging medicine he was taking must be putting all its efforts in reversing the damage of his joints, in which case, he did not mind, as it allowed him to be considerably more self-reliant at ninety-six, especially given his chronic arthritic disease. Fifteen years had passed since Michael saw his son; he was ready to reunite.

The last time was when, as a new postgraduate, at twenty-two, David decided to visit them in person after four years studying on Earth. He'd stayed a month before returning to Earth to finish his doctoral program in biology and engineering at a very prestigious university. After his completion, David promised he'd return, but the unexpectedness of life crept up on him, anchoring him on Earth permanently. He found love and quickly made a family. He was offered a lucrative position at a research laboratory owned by one of the leading pharmaceutical corporations, specializing in regenerative medicine, and with one providential stroke of genius, he made a great discovery, pushing up the ranks in the industry, becoming a self-made millionaire overnight. The board of directors subsequently offered him a position as their chairman. Taking the title, he led them like a maverick, investing, acquiring, and executing successful venture capitalist endeavors, thereby bolstering and expanding the company and himself to billionaire status. He then took all his wealth and invested it, of his accord, into research and development, starting up his own ventures. In collaboration with other entities in various fields of medicine, they were able to perfect human tissue regeneration, ending the dread of human frailty. No longer would one fear accidental amputation or irreversible organ damage. Now the panacea of human medicine was a step closer to being complete, and death and maiming had, essentially, become obsolete; only if one wanted to die—or in the unfortunate cases, such as sudden trauma or murder—would it make an appearance.

Now, at thirty-seven, David was running for public office. On top of the billions he made for himself, he also gained the reputation of being a great philanthropist, donating most of his wealth and investing in technologies that made mankind self-reliant. Instead of humankind wasting its energy to gather sustenance, they were free to pursue higher and more meaningful endeavors and purposes. Human citizens from Earth and as far as Titan were so thankful for the benefits David's life work produced; he was adulated and granted the trust of the public so much that he was spurred to run for Head Council of the Interplanetary Government. Humanity was certain a leader with such altruistic character and knowledge would usher the cosmos into a new golden age—the possibilities innumerable.

"Mom, Dad, it's nice to see you!" he said, embracing his parents under the main entrance doorway. After going through the formal pleasantries of introducing his wife, Monica, and their three children, his parents insisted they come in.

"Gentlemen, if you would, I'd prefer you all stay outside. I'd like to reunite with my family in privacy," David said, ordering his government-appointed guards, reassuring them there were no dangers inside.

Scanning the open living area, David detected minute changes, which was hard to spot, other than a minor rearrangement of furniture or an upgrade here and there; everything was left exactly like it was from his last visit. It was late morning, time beginning to transition to noon, and lunch had started taking residence in their minds. Michael and Lucy called in their posterity from the living room when the meal they had prepared was complete. Politics, diplomacy, campaign strategy, and talks of peace were discussed at the dining table, but the main focus of dialogue was about keeping current with one another and retrospection. While in communion, Michael and Lucy locked eyes from the ends of the table, signaling to each other, without saying a word, how proud they were to bear a family like theirs. How, through all the sequential order of life's forward motion, hardships and all, life brought them to this point, reaping the benefits they toiled for so diligently, producing a legacy to hold with immodest pride—a proud pinnacle of achievement they, fortunately, both had the pleasure of witnessing and sharing together.

Though they knew the effervescence would soon be gone, they made the most of it when they could, eventually bidding goodbye to David and his family on the threshold of the entryway.

"I already miss them," Lucy told Michael while they watched them take off into the distance.

"He's a busy man, Lucy. He's putting others before himself. You gotta admire that in him. We have to let him be a man—independent and free to pursue what he feels is necessary in his heart. But don't worry about feeling down, babe, because we're going to Olympus Mons in less than a month. Aren't you excited? I know you've been wanting to climb it for a long time now."

"Michael."

"Yes?"

"It's all very noble of him. But . . . he will always be my baby boy. I worry for him, too. You know how many people he'll put out of business—how many industries he and his business partners destroyed. You heard him over lunch!"

"He'll be fine."

"And my grandchildren . . . I already love them as my own. I wish they could have stayed. I could have kept them safe here."

"I think they'll be safer with those guards. Did you see how large they were?"

"Now is not the time for jokes, Michael."

"Sorry, sweetheart. I'm not trying to make you feel bad. I'm just trying to lighten your worry."

"Only a mother can understand what it feels like to worry for their children," she said with a heartfelt sigh.

Michael wrapped his arms around Lucy to comfort her and emphatically reassure her that they would see them soon. "Time will go by like that," Michael said, snapping his fingers.

Olympus Mons was the crown achievement for Lucy. Ever since she was a young adult, before meeting Michael, she was an avid mountain climber, having climb every mountain on Mars during her sixty-five years of life. The weeks leading up to the trip were ordinary and routine. Early in the morning, Michael and Lucy, having been retired for a few years, would start their day with a morning walk. Lucy, being thirty-one years younger than Michael, would with high energy and enthusiasm, keep Michael young in spirit in his old age. She would lead, help, and encourage Michael out of bed with persuasive incentives, kissing him if he'd accompany her, which he'd gladly give into. After forty-one years of marriage, he was still romantically in love with the woman he'd once repressed his feelings for. He laughed and thought it silly how, had he let his insecurity swallow him up at the time, they'd probably not be together, and had he given in earlier, they would most likely be sharing a full forty-two years of marriage. *Who knows*, he thought. But he was just glad to be by her side. Her beauty had not faded. He stared at her, seeing the orange hue from the sun shining and matching her hair as they sat at a bench facing the Valles Marineris. She caught wind of his deep glance from her periphery, began to smile, then laughed, and it spread to Michael. He told her he loved her, and she responded, "You old fool," and kissed him as promised.

An average afternoon usually consisted of leisurely going about Minerva and the surrounding regions, for lunch, recreation, or just to stroll around, driving with the roof open, letting the breeze tickle their skin as they enjoyed the sights of diverse city blocks. If they couldn't decide on an activity, they'd flip a coin for which of the two closet points of interest to visit. The spontaneity of the coin toss and the willingness to fully commit to the outcome, no matter how enjoyable or regretful it was, made it so there was never a dull afternoon between them. Michael was glad the unpredictability landed them at a miniature golf course. A fun and delightful place, unlike the previous Friday's loathsome visit to city hall regarding a new proposed ordinance to upgrade the city's trash management to a more efficient disposal system. Michael had very much liked to smash his head in with the ceremonial gavel the administrator wielded every time a new person took the floor. Snapping out of that dreadful experience, it was his turn to swing on the 18th hole. With one stroke, he made the shot from about thirty yards away, obstacles and all. After he was done gloating, as a consolation prize, Michael told Lucy he'd like to take them out dancing at the promenade for the weekend before the big trip, and she accepted.

Tossing their glasses of wine into the air, they toasted each other in celebration of their dinner arriving. In the middle of the Martian summer, air was temperate as they dined outside on the restaurant's waterfront. Gusts of wind coming from the Valles would periodically come in, offering a refreshing breeze, swaying any loose objects suspended in the air. The wine's dilating properties intensified every brush of contact the breeze made on their skin, sending shivers up Lucy's exposed spine, goosebumps appearing while they danced at breath's length. In their revelry, all other sensations were stimulated and evident by the rush of blood that reached their cheeks and Lucy's collarbone. The music playing, breeze, and sensual dancing, all compiled together, reigniting their passion. As each second passed, looking intently into one another's eyes, they found it difficult to contain themselves.

They followed up dancing with walking along the waterfront trail. After the span of several meters, they found themselves in a public square, with lit trees and shops; the stone pavement they stood on was multicolored, with square, patterned designs. The path they were on reached a bifurcation point that split into two paths, one to a view of the water and buildings along and across the river and one leading to the center of the esplanade. They'd decided on the former and spent time sitting on a bench near a large fountain. With the enthusiasm of children, they stared in wonder at the lustrous array of iridescent lights, emanating from all angles, surrounding their field of view like a lit coliseum. Buildings shined and dazzled, pedestrians whizzed by, street performers carried their acts, cyclists rode their bikes, and boats sailed on the water entering or leaving the harbors—the city was alive, and the night was only beginning.

Being led by alluring marquees and signs to guide them, Michael and Lucy eventually landed in the middle of a mall after, covering what seemed like miles of boardwalk. They hopped from shop to shop, browsing through merchandise, hoping they'd find something of interest, mostly turning up with nothing. Carrying the little they purchased, they arrived at a live theater at the top of a mezzanine floor, where a symphony was being showcased.

While waiting in line, Michael was brought into a deep contemplation. Stripping away all the advertisements, leaving only the architecture and the beauty of their shapes, and hearing all the sounds of shoppers pass by, the faint sound of dream-like background music brought up a feeling of nostalgia, making him recall the memories he and Lucy had shared over the years. Sure, they have traveled all over Mars and climbed the highest mountains, but it was in these simple moments that he felt a profound impact. These humble experiences brought their story together. He didn't know why. He couldn't quite put his finger on it. *What was triggering such longing thoughts of the past?* he thought. *Could it be the sights and sounds?* Just then, he realized what it was. He remembered the fairgrounds. In the midst of all the people, lights, and sounds, he and Lucy had shared their first kiss. He smiled. It was funny how his mind associated these things with such a beautiful moment, one of the highest moments of his life, and he laughed at the feelings it gave him, as though he had uncovered and was aware of some grand orchestration of the divine that guided and led him to this exact moment in time.

"Michael?" Lucy said, getting his attention.

"Yes," he said, snapping out of it.

"You had that droll look again—the same from last week. I'm kind of worried. I don't know if this is a cause for concern or . . ."

Michael stared at her as she voiced her concern. He drowned out her voice with the love and nostalgia residing powerfully inside him, only thinking about how much he loved her and how happy he was to be hers—and vice versa—and alive to experience it. "I'm okay, honey. I'm just so happy to be here with you. That's why I was smiling," he said. "Come on, honey, we're next in line."

Chapter 11

VACATION ON OLYMPUS MONS

BEFORE DAWN, THE tranquil sounds of insects chirping and subtle winds blowing into the dark accompanied Michael and Lucy as they rolled their luggage across their dimly lit walkway. A cab was waiting to transport them, and the driver helped place their bags inside the vehicle. Lucy asked Michael if he left anything before locking the door. Her reminder jogged his memory, making him doubt himself. He motioned to the driver and Lucy that he'd return, brushed by the leaves and shrubbery surrounding the walkway, and remembered the surprise he forgot to bring for Lucy.

In his office was a hidden storage box in one of the drawers that could only be exposed by removing the mock compartment that covered it. He had been excitedly anticipating giving Lucy the gift for weeks. He held it up to the light, staring at it. A small, heartfelt sigh came over him; looking at the rare Martian diamond ring reminded him of his soulmate. The diamond itself held only a ceremonial purpose—a statement of love for her. The ring banner was inscribed with a pattern and design constructed of dozens of words and phrases. He shed a tear when he thought of all the days and hours he spent picking the right words to sum up his love for her. He did his best. Some feelings were indescribable—absent due to a loss for words. He figured he'd reserve those unknown words to a sublime place—in a realm that transcended everyday experience.

"Sweetie, what took you so long?" Lucy asked as Michael returned to the driveway.

"Had to check every room, darling. No need to worry. No electricity will be wasted around here," Michael said, dusting his hands.

The two boarded and buckled in the cab and flew off to the airport, where they were to catch their two-hour flight to Ionia, a city that laid at the foot of Olympus Mons.

From the plane's window, Michael could see the majestic mountain in all of its glory. As the plane descended and shifted northeast toward Ionia, the peaks of the mountain were covered by the clouds. With the remaining part of the mountain fading like a trail of vapor behind the plane's tail, the landscape transitioned into the Amazonis Planitia. The plains stretched far off into the distance, past Michael's vision, allowing him to see the gradient contrast between the two terrains.

Breathing in the open air after disembarking, the city had an antiquated touch, giving Michael and Lucy the sense that they'd traveled back in time. Everything seemed to adhere to a strict building code, whether deliberately planned or not, and it looked like a rendition of an old American prairie town. Everything was uniform, in style, and even the technology was fitted to match the surroundings. Everything complemented and suited the landscape perfectly, and it brought a warm and hospitable feeling.

Catching a ride, they headed to a farmhouse located about twenty miles from the airport, where they were to lodge and stay about a week before venturing toward the mountain. On the way, they saw large fields tended by drones, modified to adhere to the aesthetic trend. The bots were plated with wood and tin, fitted with extraneous wings, like an invention of Da Vinci. And to give more authenticity, the machines creaked when they moved. Many farms had windmills and obsolete buildings serving only as mementos of times past, back when they held a purpose. Michael and Lucy enjoyed every minute of it. For too long, they were accustomed to city life, and the steampunk environment provided an escape from the constant bombardment of stimuli they experienced back home. This long, uninterrupted country sky had a way of slowing down the pace, giving them a higher sense of awareness to fully immerse in the experience of everything around them.

"It's so beautiful here, Michael," Lucy said, reclining on a chair outside the farmhouse, facing the mountain range.

The fields were fertile, covered in rich green grass, with other vibrant colors emanating from a multitude of flowers that they could not name without the aid of their interface. The scene looked like the sky had showered the ridge and valleys with the finest paints. Each hue blended and contoured in harmony, never overpowering or encroaching another flowers' space, only transitioning at the appropriate points. It provided a breathtaking view when the winds picked up, swaying the vegetation of the land in a synchronized groove, highlighting its exuberance.

"It's amazing how, just beyond the horizon, on the other side of the valley, it's all desert," Michael responded. "We better enjoy this while we can before all we see is sand for who knows how long," he said, laughing.

Time spent doing nothing at the farmhouse whisked by, and the long expedition to tour Olympus Mons was underway. Foreseeing the obstacles and challenges they'd come across, the Acostas carried an exo-suit tailored for Michael so he could enjoy the trip. The suit wrapped around the backside of his body, including his arms and legs. Its carbon backbone was tailored specifically for him and was further stabilized with a buckle that wrapped around his waist, giving him the freedom to maneuver around, unhindered in all directions, and allowing him the strength to endure the long-haul.

"I can't help but feel a little self-conscious using this instead of walking and climbing with you," Michael said with a long face.

"Honey, you know you have nothing to be ashamed of," she said, caressing his face while fastening him inside the suit. The loving affirmation reassured the old man, and it gave him the virility to yank out of his self-loathing. "Need a hand with that?" he asked, pointing at a bag on the floor. "You know I do."

They checked out of the farmhouse with all their belongings hanging off Michael's new augmented backside—and all of it fitting conveniently in one giant bag. They were met with favorable conditions outside.

She replied, "Let's get going."

Crossing through the trails in the valleys, there was life teeming everywhere. There were rare sightings—plants and creatures they had never seen.

Michael lived on Mars for a lifetime, and though he was originally from Earth, he felt the new life around him was truly alien. Even Lucy, a native to Mars, found the new trove of flora and fauna peculiar and foreign. Browsing through flowers, they saw insects of all colors and shapes crawling, flying, and scattering. Some insects differed in uniqueness, an extra segmented body or an additional set of legs or eyes, but there were others that further captured their attention. Like the flowers, these insects were colored from all ends of the spectrum. A few were even rainbow-colored, a metallic effect that unintentionally mirrored the reflections of everything surrounding them. Michael could see a shadow cast into a large butterfly, and the shadow above kept moving. He looked up and realized it was a large bird. He didn't know if it was a kind of hawk or eagle, as the environment seemed to modify this creature and give it its own distinguishing traits. Captivated by the majestic creature, he saw that the sun was high in the sky, which prompted him to check the time. "Honey, let's go," he said. "We still have some ground to cover."

A few hours before dusk, five days later, they arrived at a post at the end of the trail. The station was located where the elevation began to climb at the mountain's base—intermediate from lustrous green valley to dry, gritty chaparral. The edifice and change in surroundings implied an informal welcoming landmark that greeted Michael and Lucy to the start of the anticipated lengthy peregrination. They entered the station and asked the ranger if he could guide them to the nearest camping ground. He suggested they rent a room at an odd-looking but highly modern lodge close by, so they could settle their belongings securely and have a comfortable place to sleep. They agreed and headed there at once.

Thirty minutes later, covering a kilometer or so, they could see an oasis of light in the middle of an endless field of darkness. It was not hard to miss. The source of light lit the way, along with the stars above, illuminating the ground. The sound of rocks and dirt under their feet felt like it would continue forever, but finally, they made it within yards of the lodge, and the sound didn't seem so exaggerated anymore. The building was made of different-sized cubes, laid out in different directions, all connected through precise arrangements. The light fixtures around the building's sides and pathways emitted elongated shadows, highlighting sharp angles on the sand and distorted silhouettes of Michael and Lucy extending their hands for the entrance doors.

Their minds stood frozen as they looked around, enthralling them on their way to the front desk. The ceilings and walls of the lobby seemed to stretch out indefinitely; the builder was precise and careful when planning the layout. Its cathedral-like nature was the cause for the tingling sensation shooting throughout Michael's body. Decadence was the motto. The lobby was adorned with futuristic, luxury décor. The level of detail and interest emitting from the designs and amenities was high, even higher in entertainment value. *Who knew one could have this much style out here in the desert?* Michael thought. The fixed combinations had an effect on them. It even exceeded the limits when Michael—still hypnotized—bumped into the counter; the receptionist let out an artificial chuckle and welcomed them.

In their spacious suite, the attendants dropped Michael and Lucy's belongings. Michael second-guessed whether they'd packed enough or if the hotel was over-accommodating.

"Guess they're used to people who only travel with their entire wardrobes," Michael said, laughing at his own joke.

In the living room, the extent to astonish guests with larger-than-life extravagance did not stop. The furniture catered to one's whims, but outside, they were treated with a view incomparable to any other place. The wall was a pane of glass that showered from the ceiling to the floor, covering end to end at the beams. Drawing close to the window, the glare reflecting from inside started to fade, and outside, they could see as far as Phobos. Underneath, brightened by artificial and heavenly means, a private area laid waiting. The area was closed off and private but not too over-restrictive, showing just enough scenery while blocking anyone or anything attempting to pry. A fluorescent pool gave off a turquoise light, drawing Michael and Lucy in. Looking into each other's eyes, they had the same thought; piece by piece, they left their clothing scattered behind them.

The next day came. Lucy—too comfortable to move—awoke and decided it was time to rise out of bed and begin the day. She pulled down the sheets covering her head that she used to block the sunlight, allowing her to sleep beyond early daybreak. The movement was swift, matching the eagerness she felt to greet Michael. Facing her right side, she saw Michael sleeping, curled up in multiple layers of blankets. She found it humorous, tapping and nudging the large mound. Tossing the covers back, she could see he was not there. Puzzled, she wondered where her husband could be. Lucy swiveled and slid off the bed.

"Michael?" she yelled while advancing into the living area.

Darting her eyes, surveying the place, she noticed a red rose and card on the floor next to the door. The note read, "Please follow the trail of rose petals I left out. Follow until you see the only large, withered tree, just behind the dune in the back. I'll explain everything. There, I will be waiting. Love, Michael."

Lucy wasted no time complying to her husband's wishes. She

searched through a scene of disorganization to find and fasten her shoes. She locked up and headed out, starting at the initial petal that stood at the end of the pool. After unhinging the gate, the other petals of the trail were spaced out in ten-foot increments. On the way there, Lucy thought about what Michael had planned. She knew this trip coincided with their fortieth anniversary and that this was Michael's gift to her, but as to why he would drag her to sandy clay was a mystery. The thought stirred a little excitement inside her. The outline of the tree and Michael became more vivid as she approached closer. The sun gave them a glistening glow from the heat haze. The search for her husband was finally over.

"What's with all the secrecy?" Lucy said.

"Glad you asked. Mind standing right here, underneath this bare tree?" he said, pointing. "I can see that you're confused, but if you bear with me a moment, it'll all make sense. I've brought you here to get away from anything that could distract me from presenting you this gift. Lucy, I've been meaning to give you this for a while and found the perfect opportunity in this place. It was already planned to give you this for our anniversary, but I just didn't know when or where, but my god, I thought it so fitting to do so here."

He pulled the ring from his pocket, removed it from its case, and placed it on her finger. She gasped, letting out tears.

"Before you, I was much like this tree right here. Alone, withering away, just a fragmented life in a vast desert sea. But everything changed when you came into my life. You were the spark of light that gave me sustenance, much like the sun did to this tree in its prime.

"Everywhere I went, I felt like I didn't belong—I felt like an alien, just wandering endlessly and finding no rest. I felt betrayed and abandoned by the world. But when you came, you made me feel like I belonged, like I was deserving of life after feeling so worthless. I lived a veiled existence filled with monotony.

"Life lacked value. There were no sights or sounds; life was lackluster and without songs. But you—you colored the world and sang with every word you spoke. You allowed me to feel every spectrum of emotion and gave life its richness.

"There was always devotion in your eyes and sincerity in your smile. You were always eager to help me, and you were never ashamed because of me.

"But above all, you gave me something that everyone in the universe deserves—you gave me love. And that is what this ring symbolizes.

"The design around the ring is words to express how I feel about you. It's an account and testament of my love and gratitude for you, though you cannot see with the naked eye. Wherever you go, my breath is with you. I love you, Lucy."

They held each other. Saturated deeply in their love, their embrace lasted several minutes. A sudden wind picked up and shook an almost severed branch from the tree, jolting them out of their moment.

"Honey, we better start going. I can remember that shadow from the tree was a bit lower before," Lucy said.

"You're right. I can see you turning a little red," Michael said, poking fun at Lucy.

They headed back, deciding to spend the rest of the day at the inn and wait for the following day's expedition.

Michael had more breakfast as Lucy went over the plans. He reassured her, through his mouthful, not to worry about the logistics of the trip. "Lucy, we'll be fine. We've got everything we need," he said.

Burning through many kilometers of trails and pathways, the couple reached about 16,000 meters from the base in the span of eighty days. On the way, they encountered a group of hiking enthusiasts also on their way to the summit. Michael and Lucy found the extra company encouraging and informative. One member of the group, Taylor, had already climbed the mountain years ago. She acted as an unofficial guide, telling Michael and Lucy everything they'd come to expect. With the air getting thinner, they strapped on their oxygen cannulas so they wouldn't faint as the elevation rose higher.

The ground no longer generated anything living, at least as far as the naked eye could tell—total bareness. The sun's intensity became overwhelming and the air frigid. The climb would be impossible without sufficient technology protecting against extreme elements.

"What's this about?" Michael asked, pointing at a post. The sign was eye-catching and alarming. It read, "In case of emergency, use vent for cover."

"Don't you worry," Taylor reassured. "These things are just here in case of an accident."

"Like?" Lucy asked.

"On rare occasions, there have been avalanches and sandstorms that were pretty devastating. So, these were made as a preventive measure. Don't worry. We'll be fine. Didn't you guys see the other signs earlier?" Taylor said.

"No. I guess we were too in the moment to realize," Michael said.

"You two relax. There hasn't been one of those in like fifty years," she said.

Convinced but a bit shaken, Michael and Lucy decided to continue with the group.

The selection of trails became limited, and the crew had to cross over several burdensome crags. On one crossing, they were all presented with a clear view below. Looking down, they could see the mountain sprouting up from the clouds. It was a spectacular sight. There was a feeling of the divine; they recounted old myths and legends of the god's heavenly abodes they'd read about.

"It sure looks like everyone's idea of what heaven would look like," said one of the crewmates.

Lucy responded, "Funny how it gives the illusion you could walk on the clouds."

A hundred days in and twenty kilometers above ground, another two thousand meters stood in the way of reaching the zenith. The modes for getting there had become more difficult and steeper to overcome. Every obstacle was riddled with danger. Michael's exo-suit was proving to be inadequate the higher they went. The impasses had come to be so challenging, preventing Michael from going any further. Lucy would finally convince him to head back down after many failed attempts. She gently reassured him that they would meet him soon, only ten days from the peak. He complied. On stable ground, just a few yards below, he waved to the crew as they started climbing upward. His heart ached when his wife waved from above. *Now came the hard part, enduring the journey all alone*, he thought. Without company, the elements seemed to amplify in their severity. He counted the day's remaining—a hundred, eighty-five, sixty-two; then, by around 12,000 meters, he considered heading back to meet them. "No!" he shouted, reminding himself to stick to the plan. But longing for Lucy crept inside.

The air at 4,000 meters was still, quiet, and warm. Michael could saturate his lungs to full capacity. With his surroundings less intense, he was given more time to freely observe it all. The reappearance of animals was a contrast from before, but of course, an arid desert could only provide so much for him to view. Tiny critters scurried along the ground with the intention of finding food. And above, a bird resembling an owl waited to devour an unfortunate victim. In the far distance below, a small herd of hooved animals congregated next to what was without question a familiar place. To do nothing but gather himself was the plan—do nothing and just watch.

Thoughts of Lucy ran in Michael's mind. He wondered how she was faring after eighty days of not seeing her. *How many miles was she behind?* Not wanting to overthink, he brushed the thoughts to the side. He must've slipped inside his own head for a while, wrestling thoughts, because as he was getting ready to head down again, it appeared much later in the day than he previously saw from the afternoon sun. Not only that, but there was a faint feeling in the air that something had changed. There were no animals, and the ones he noticed before were farther in the distance, fleeing away or hiding. He looked up. The sky still had enough daylight left. *What could account for the sudden change?* he thought. Picking up a stronger ominous touch, some intuitive feeling inside him kept nagging him. Drowning with concern, he decided to go back toward Lucy—hoping to silence the worry.

Chapter 12

THE SANDS OF TIME

NO SIGNAL. ALL communication was down as Michael hoped his interface could reach Lucy. At this height, much less Lucy's—wherever that was—any form of communication was inconceivable. *She couldn't be more than a couple days away if they were coming back on schedule*, he thought. But each minute and meter seemed to extend and loop into an unattainable, timeless void, and his optimism wavered. His clock read fifteen minutes after his initial start back, but it felt like hours. His distance said he traveled several meters, but it seemed he never left. And he was growing more impatient. He wished his body was suited to tackle the challenges of the trip. Had he been able, there would have been no need to separate from Lucy, no need for this anxiety. His impatience turned into frustration. He was frustrated that his rheumatic joints prevented him from using the suit's full capacities that could have propelled him faster. But amid the anger, there was hope. There was still plenty of daylight left and energy inside him and the suit to power through another voyage.

A total of twenty minutes passed, and the excessive thoughts were long gone, replaced with the cadence of his steps. His legs' repetitive movement up and down, pulling up the dirt underneath with each swing, sustained his hypnotic, distractible state. His interface alerted him that his vitals were low and he needed water. Having passed a rest stop minutes before, not wanting to turn around, he figured he'd wait to refill his canteen at the next one, about eight minutes forward. Thirst wasn't a sensation he was feeling, but he was cold from the wind.

Debris of sand and other matter began to lightly glide downhill, forming undulating patterns against Michael's arduous uphill climb. The sand oscillated around his feet, chaotically moving in relation to the unstable gusts of wind, intensifying with each second. He blew a breath of air into his hands and rubbed them, hoping it would generate more heat to withstand the cooler temperature. Taking a break from looking at the trail, he shifted his head upward, glancing ahead. He checked the time again; only ninety seconds had elapsed. And again, the winds picked up, and the sand followed. *Why has time stood still? Why have the conditions turned unfavorable?* Michael thought. Not wanting to stop, he knew the rest stop was a little further.

A fog of sand covered the mountain, and visibility was nonexistent. The winds reached the tipping point of normal range, blowing Michael and the sand violently in a maelstrom. Almost a minute in, Michael began to feel stuck in a state of inertness. He knew he was traveling upward, but he could not pinpoint his location. With no reference, it felt as though he was wandering through the darkness in a futile attempt to look for anything to grab that might help guide him toward shelter. He knew he was in the middle of a sandstorm— how severe was unknown. To weather the storm, it was vital to find an emergency bunker—fast. The urgency was reinforced as his body gave off signs of danger from potential threats. Elevated heart rate, heavy breathing, losing his train of thought—through the turbulence and confusion, his mind seemed to focus on reuniting with Lucy. That thought made it possible for him to keep enduring.

Cause for concern was raised. The winds became more violent and strong and began to deviate Michael off course. He could not tell anymore which direction he was going—if he was going downhill or up. At times, the gusts knocked him down. Every time it happened, he would pick himself off and resist the urge to give up. He checked the time, and only seconds had passed; through this hell, every second felt like minutes. The howls of rushing wind became louder and made the storm more intimidating. In the distance, he thought he heard a cry for his name. *It couldn't be*, he thought. Again, he heard what he thought was Lucy calling out his name in the far-off distance. He stopped, turning his body toward the cry once more. Not thinking twice, he headed toward the sound, knowing, without a doubt, it was his wife.

"How's he looking, Doctor?"

"It's hard to tell. Your father is deep in a coma. When we found him, we were surprised he survived the impact, based on his injuries—let alone the amount of time he was out there. Something tells me it's not just the machines sustaining him. There's a reason he's still holding on. All we can do is wait. If anything, just call. I'm sorry, Mr. Acosta."

David did not know how to take in the doctor's words, but he found a semblance of comfort in him trying to be optimistic for the family. The prognosis did accent the room, though, and matched its lifeless, cold foundations.

Activity rung throughout the whole hospital and could be felt. Nurses went from room to room, checking on patients and scrambling through the halls, and the machines beating for his father felt like one giant orchestration of machines in clockwork. Seeing his father lie motionless was upsetting. And as time went by, it became a little more difficult to turn toward him. The news of patients recovering and the sound of commotion became unbearable. Knowing it was irrational, it almost felt as if his father was being singled out and excluded from the collective miracles circulating the hospital. The doctor's words and the events that happened so quickly to his family rang in David's mind as the television resumed broadcast of the sandstorm that occurred on Olympus Mons. How was his father going to pull through? And if he pulled through, how was he going to tell his father all that happened?

"One hundred people are dead, and several remain in critical condition after last week's sandstorm at Olympus Mons and the surrounding regions. Experts estimate that winds reached up to 177 kilometers per hour—the worst in recent years—which caused for widespread destruction around the plains. Rescuers and authorities have informed us that many search efforts are still underway, as they believe many more are out there..."

Being reminded by the news was another emotional blow. Weeping at his father's side and still in the throes of mourning, how would he tell his father that, of those 100 dead, his mother—the love of his father's life—was among them? He groaned, pleading to his father to pull through. Monica, sensing the unimaginable pain David was going through, crept in the room, despite David telling her he wanted to be alone. Seeing her husband, a man being primed to lead the known solar system, in this way was startling. She comforted him by placing his head on her bosom, knowing that even the most valiant and principled men needed comfort at times like these. As David seemed to drift off in his wife's arms, Michael, in his halfway state, fencing between the realms of the living and the dead, was still searching for his Lucy.

Deep and far in an intangible elsewhere, where his conscious thought existed, he never left the mountain, still climbing uphill in search of his wife. The call for his name was all but a farce when the dust had settled. Nonetheless, he didn't allow his unmet expectation of Lucy on the other end to discourage him. With the storm cleared, he found new optimism and strength to continue searching. The conditions on the mountain resumed to normalcy despite the brief setback. It was imperative that Michael capitalize as much ground as possible before sunset.

At the rest stop, he found it odd that he wasn't thirsty—or tired—like he thought he was. Not wanting to think too much of it, he chalked it up to his body being in fight mode.

Days seemed to pass, without a trace of Lucy anywhere, but a week later, Michael started to see figures coming toward him. And in an instant, a sudden jolt of wind propelled Michael upward. Getting closer, he could feel the warm energy only Lucy could emit. He knew it was her. They locked together, smiling and looking deep in each other's eyes. The longing built up from the days and months that separated them poured out in the tears. Their hearts echoed loudly; their counterpart was within reach. It was not just their bodies that reunited but their essence—the deep, innate, untraceable soul in the body that became one again. And they brought it all into culmination with a kiss.

"I love you," Lucy said, breaking away. Michael's reply mirrored. "I will always love you, no matter where I go."

"Huh? Honey, what are you talking about? You're right here. I'm right here. We're here together, and I promise you, I'll never make the mistake of separating from you ever again!"

She was reluctant to say his name.

"What is it, Lucy?" he said with a worried look.

She dared not look at him and told him that she must go.

"Where are you going? Where do you have to go? Answer me, please."

As he pleaded with her, she dissipated like the sand that blew across the desert floor. The other hikers soon followed. He was alone. "What happened?" he asked himself. Had he not been astonished, he would have cried out in pain and despair.

There was a feeling stirring up in him, gravitating him toward the sun. Without a single word, he knew everything. The knowledge imparted by an unknown source told him what was going on in the world—calling him back. Michael was given the choice to return or join Lucy and stardust. He knew what awaited at home. He thought about his son, his daughter-in-law, and his grandchildren. Conflicted and confused, he asked himself deeper questions, going over every aspect of their lives and how they would be affected by his absence. He deliberated until he had reached his decision. He knew his family would always be taken care of. *How many more years of life did I really have left?* he thought. *And how long could I endure a life without my wife? But on the contrary, how grand would the devastation be for my son to endure the loss of both parents, burying us both? What value could I give to my grandchildren?* Just as he was sure of his decision, he second-guessed, torn between opposing ends pulling him in opposite directions.

"He's crashing again. Quick, get the paddles!"

The doctors, in a frenzy, were doing all they could to restart Michael's heart.

"He knows she's gone," David said. While waiting for the next jolt of electricity to enter his father, David bent down. He whispered into Michael's ear, "Go, Dad. Go to Mom, Dad. She's waiting for you."

"Clear!" said the on-call doctor.

"He's not responding," yelled another.

David saw the look of disappointment on the doctor's faces as they prepared to break the bad news. He knew what was coming and was not upset.

After waiting for the chaos to settle, Monica hugged David.

"I'm so sorry, honey. I can't imagine what you must be going through," she said.

He lifted his head up from her embrace and smiled, telling her, "Don't worry about me. If there's one thing I know about those two, not even death will separate them. In my heart, I know he is happily with my mother, and I'm glad he made that choice to be with her again. He's in heaven with his beloved wife, whom he loved with his whole being—a love I hope to measure up to one day with you. And I will miss them both very much."

"You already measure up, baby. Your parents gave you the best example of love and how it should be, and I am proud they raised you to be the man I've fallen madly in love with. Let's go, honey," Monica said. "We need to check on the kids."

Just before they left Michael's room, David reached over his father to give him a final hug. Upon returning to Monica, she noticed David's attention fixated on his right hand, balled up and carrying something.

"What is it?" she asked.

"It's a ring. One of the attending nurses gave it to me earlier. Apparently, it was my mother's. I've never seen her wear it, though. Must've been new, from the looks of it." He sighed. "I can tell this ring is special," he said, looking toward Monica's direction. "I know that whatever life throws our way, we'll be like this ring—intact and one."

www.ingramcontent.com/pod-product-compliance
Lightning Source LLC
LaVergne TN
LVHW041611070526
838199LV00052B/3099